ALIEN MINDS

By
E. EVERETT EVANS

I0616802

ARMCHAIR FICTION
PO Box 4369, Medford, Oregon 97504

WHO LURKS IN THE MINDS OF ALIENS?

George Hanlon was a gifted secret operative for the Inter-Stellar Corps—he could read minds and control them. Unfortunately, and understandably, alien minds were far more vexing.

The Federation of Planets had invited Estrella to join as a full-fledged equal member. And while the Estrellans may not have been as technologically advanced as those of Earth, their ethics and ability to live together in peace transcended anything humankind had ever known.

But there were forces afoot that sought to block Estrella from joining. Crimes—of a sort previously unknown to the Estrellan natives—began occurring, and the Federation was taking the rap. Who was at the bottom of this propaganda war? That is what George Hanlon and his team needed to find out…on the planet of Alien Minds.

CAST OF CHARACTERS

GEORGE HANLON
This cocky young captain could really get inside your mind—literally, but he was soon challenged in ways he never imagined.

ADMIRAL NEWTON
A savvy admiral in the Inter-Stellar Corps, he was also Hanlon's father and leader of the Estrella investigation team.

INO YANDOR
This theatrical agent and racketeer found himself in the unenviable position of being used to discredit the Federation.

ELUS AMIR
He was the wise and just Ruler of Estrella, whose shoulders bore a monumental decision that would forever affect his world.

ADWAL IRAD
Once an intelligent and sound choice for Second-in-Line, he suddenly changed—but what was behind his bizarre behavior?

THE BEING
A strange and powerful psychic entity of unknown origins, whose interests in Estrella were most pronounced—but why?

CHAPTER ONE

"WERE YOU LOOKING FOR A ROCH, NYER?" AN oily voice spoke up just by the elbow of George Hanlon. "I have some excellent ones here, sir."

"Yes, nyer. I want several, if I can find ones to suit me," the young man replied. Nor could anyone, glancing at him, know he was not a native of this planet, Szstruyyah, which the Inter-Stellar Corpsmen, in self-defense, called "Estrella." For the cosmetic-specialist who handled the secret servicemen's disguises had done a marvelous job in transforming the blond young Corpsman into an Estrellan native.

Hanlon continued looking into the outside cages containing these tailless roches, the Estrellan equivalent of wild dogs. "I want eight, all as near the same size, coloring and age as possible."

"Eight, did you say?" the merchant looked at him in astonishment. Hanlon, carefully reading the surface of the man's mind, sensed the conflict there between the ethics his religion and philosophy had taught him, his natural love of haggling, and a desire to make as much profit as possible. But he could not sense the slightest suspicion that the man confronting him was not another Estrellan.

This was a great relief to Hanlon, for he was still afraid he might be recognized as a stranger and an alien. In his disguise he was still humanoid in shape, and still his five feet eleven inches in height. But in addition to the ragged beard and longish hair, he had undergone outward structural differences that made him seem almost totally unhuman.

"That's right. Eight. I want them to be about two years old, in good health. Can you supply them?"

"I can if you can pay for them," the native looked somewhat questioningly at Hanlon's cheap clothing.

The young secret serviceman smiled, and jingled coins in his pocket. "I can pay."

"Then come with me, nyer, and we will find the ones you want."

Hanlon followed him inside the peculiar little open-faced stall that was one of the hundreds surrounding the great market square of this city of Stearra, largest on the West Continent of Estrella. His nose wrinkled against the stench of the unclean kennels.

The roches, seeing a stranger and, perhaps, being somewhat upset by his strange, alien effluvia, set up the peculiar, frenzied yelping that was their customary sound. To Hanlon, it was reminiscent of the wail of earthly coyotes.

The young Corpsman was on a very hair-trigger of caution and tenseness. Despite his splendid disguise, he had plodded through the crowd of the market place with a great deal of trepidation.

He had seemingly come through all right so far, and he began to relax a bit, yet was still somewhat fearful that he might give himself away by some difference of action, or speech, or by breaking one of their customs or taboos about which he knew all too little, despite his briefing and study before coming here.

"Have you decided which ones you want, nyer?" the proprietor asked, waving his hand toward the various cages, hardly able to believe he was to make such a large sale.

Hanlon said nothing, continuing to scan closely the roches, for his thoughts were still very much on this, his first prolonged venture into the streets and among the crowds of this strange new world to which he had been assigned on his second problem.

His mind was constantly contacting others, for George Spencer Newton Hanlon was the only member of the secret service who was at all able to read minds. But he could read only their surface thoughts—and these Estrellans had such peculiar mental processes, so different from those of the humans with whom he was familiar, that they were almost non-understandable.

So he was still a bit hesitant to start the bickering he knew he must engage in to stay in character. To delay a bit further he continued examining the animals in the cages, not only with his eyes but mentally scanning the brain of each, that he might be sure of finding those in perfect health, with minds he could most easily control.

"Though how I can expect to find healthy ones in a filthy dump like this, I don't know," he thought. But he finally did.

While he was doing this, however, he was reminded of the time he had discovered this ability to "read" animal minds, and how his subsequent studies had enabled him to control their minds and bodily actions with amazing skill. It was this ability that had led him to this market place on his unusual quest.

"I'll take that one, and that, and that," he said at last, pointing out, one after another the eight animals he wanted.

"Yes, nyer, yes," the puzzled but delighted proprietor said, as he transferred the indicated animals to a single, large cage. "That will cost you..." He eyed Hanlon carefully to see if he could get away with an exorbitant price, something seemed to tell him the stranger did not know just how much roches customarily sold for, and he decided to raise his asking price considerably. "...they will be seven fine pentas each, nyer, and believe me, you are getting a fine price. I usually get ten each..." He was lucky to get two Hanlon read in his mind. "...but since this is such a large sale I can afford to make you a bargain."

Hanlon grinned to himself as he computed quickly. Five iron pentas, he knew, made one copper penta, five coppers one tin penta, five of these one silver penta, and five silvers a gold one. This made the silver piece worth about one-half a Federation credit. The price seemed ridiculously low, even with this big mark-up. Hanlon would willingly have paid it, but he had learned from the briefing tapes, and again now from his reading of this merchant's mind, that they loved to haggle over their sales—made a sort of game of it—so he turned away, registering disgust.

"A fool you think me, perhaps," he said witheringly. "Seven silver pentas, indeed. One would be a great price for such ill-fed, scrawny, pitiable animals as those."

The merchant raised his hands and voice in simulated rage—which did not prevent him from running around to face Hanlon's retreating figure, and bar his way. "'Robber', he calls me, then tries to rob me in turn. Six?" he suggested hopefully.

Hanlon was now enjoying the game, and threw himself into it with vigor. "I call on Zappa to witness that you are, indeed, the worst thief unhung," he also spoke loudly, angrily, largely for the benefit of the crowd of natives that was swiftly gathering to watch and listen to this sport. "Look, that one is crooked of leg, this one's hair is ready to fall out, that one is fifteen years old if a day. I'll give you two."

Yet he knew all the animals were in perfect health, and all about two years old. He had carefully selected only such.

"I ask anyone here," the seller wailed as he waved toward the crowd that was watching and listening with huge enjoyment, "I ask anyone here who knows roches to examine these you have chosen. They are all exceptional, all perfect. The best in my shop. Five and a half."

Hanlon turned away again. "I'll go find an *honest* dealer," he started to push through the crowd, but the merchant hurried after him and grasped his smock. "Wait, nyer, wait. It breaks my heart to do this. I'll lose a month's profit, but I'll sell them to you for five pentas each. To my best friend I wouldn't give a better price."

"That shows why you have no friends. Three even, take it or leave it," Hanlon was still pretending indifference.

"I'm ruined; I'll be forced out of business," the dealer screamed. "They cost me more than that. Oh why did I rise this morning. Give me four?"

Hanlon grinned and dug out a handful of the pentagonal-shaped gold and silver pieces. He counted into the merchant's quivering but dirty hands the agreed-upon thirty-two pentas.

The native looked at them, wordlessly, but his face was a battleground of mixed emotions. Finally he reluctantly counted out half of them into his other hand, and held them out to Hanlon. "No, nyer, I cannot over-charge you. Two is the price."

"You're an honest man after all, and I apologize," Hanlon said, smiling, as he pushed back the outstretched hand. "Those I chose are fine animals, perfect, and the best in your shop. So keep the money. Send them to my room this midday," he commanded. "It's on the street of the Seven Moons, at the corner of the street of the Limping Caval—the house painted pink in front. Second floor to the rear. My name—Gor Anlo—is on the door."

He had taken that name on this planet since it most nearly corresponded to his own from among the common Estrellan names.

The roch-dealer, well pleased with the outcome, bobbed obsequiously. "It shall be done as you say, nyer, and I shall include feeding and drinking dishes. What about food for them?"

"That's right, they'll need dishes, and thank you. Let's see your meat." But after examining the poor quality food the merchant displayed, he would not buy.

"I'll get something elsewhere, if this is the best you have," Hanlon told the man with a disarming smile. "Such fine roches deserve the best."

"Yes, my food is poor," the dealer moved his hand deprecatingly. "I'm glad the roches are to have such a considerate master."

And Hanlon could read in his mind that the merchant actually was pleased. The SS man felt that he had passed this first public test with high grades.

In one of the better-class food stalls Hanlon found some good, clean meat, and the other foods such animals ate. After the customary game of haggling, he ordered a two days' supply to be delivered at once, and the order duplicated every other day until further notice.

Then he hunted up a suit-maker. Here it took a lot of persuasion, and the showing of his money, before the tailor would even believe that Hanlon really meant what he said when he tried to order nine uniforms, eight of them of such outlandish shape and size. For one of them was for himself, the others for his newly bought roches.

It was only when Hanlon finally lost patience and said sharply, "You stupid lout. I want them for a theatrical act, that the uniform-maker realized the reason for such an unusual order. Then things ran smoothly. The design was sketched and material of a red to harmonize with the grayish-tan of the roches was chosen. The tailor consented also, for an added fee, to rush the job...

Hanlon's way home led through part of the district where the larger, better-class shops were located. He stopped in front of one of these.

He knew from his studies and from what he had seen here that Estrella was just at the beginning of a mechanical culture. What sciences and machines they had were unbelievably crude and primitive to him, accustomed as he was to the high technologies of Terra and the colonized planets.

This display he was scanning featured their means of personal transportation. There were, of course, no moving slideways, nor even automobiles nor ground cabs nor copters. Instead, the Estrellans used motorized tricycles. Even the smallest of these was heavy, cumbersome, crude and inefficient, but they were speedier and easier than walking—when they worked.

The tricycles had large wheels, about three feet in diameter, with semi-hard, rubber-like tires. There were two wheels in back and one in front, steered by a tiller lever. Because of the weight of the engine and tank for the gas, even the smallest trike weighed several hundred pounds.

Hanlon found to his dismay that the fuel was acetylene gas. Electricity had been discovered here, but as yet they knew only direct current. No AC—no vacuum tubes—no telephones—no radios—no television. "No nothing," Hanlon snorted in disgust.

But the native scientists and technicians had found how to use their DC to manufacture calcium carbide. Thus, they had plenty of acetylene gas, and many ways of using this for power.

"I'd lots rather have a good two-wheeled bike," Hanlon thought to himself, but decided, "guess I'd better buy one of these. Probably have to do a lot of chasing around, and since there's no 'for hire' ground cabs, I don't want to have to walk all the time. Besides, I might have to get somewhere in a hurry."

The salesman had first tried to sell him one of the larger three or four-place family-sized tricycles that steered with a wheel. But Hanlon finally made the man understand that he wanted only a one-man machine, and the purchase was haggled into completion—at a price so low it surprised the young secret serviceman.

"Sure is one screwy world," he shook his head as he rode back toward his apartment, after learning how to operate his new machine and its tricky engine.

Back in his room, Hanlon reviewed the situation to date on this, his second assignment for the secret service of the Inter-Stellar Corps. He had been at the head of the commission sent to Algon where he (Hanlon) had been largely instrumental in freeing from slavery the strange, vegetable-like people, the Guddus (see *Man of Many Minds*, 1953). The commission had helped them make a treaty with the Federated Planets by which the natives allowed the humans to mine certain valuable metals from their planet, and to maintain the spaceship yards that had been built by the men who had formerly enslaved them, in return for protection from exploiters, and for certain cultural assistance. Just as his work there was about finished, a message had come for Captain Hanlon to report back to the planet Simonides.

There he met his father, Regional Admiral Newton, second in command of the secret service, (This discrepancy of names was due to the fact that after young Spencer Newton's mother died, and his father "disappeared" —at the time he joined the secret service—the boy was adopted by George Hanlon, an ex-Corpsman, and his wife, and had taken his foster father's name.)

"We're not getting anywhere on Estrella," his father had begun abruptly once they had warmly greeted each other. "I've come to the conclusion, and the Council agrees, that we need your special mental abilities there. But take it easy, Spence…er, I never can seem to get used to calling you 'George.' Don't try to go it alone…and you can wipe that cocky smirk off your face, mister," he commanded sternly. "This time it's an official order from the top brass. Those Estrellans are distinctly alien—not humans gone wrong."

Hanlon sobered down a bit, but secretly could not entirely shake off his attitude, feeling sure he was more than a match for any trouble he might run into. Hadn't he proved it, on Algon and right here on Simonides? Sure he had. Great Snyder, he wasn't a kid any more. He was a secret serviceman of the Inter-Stellar Corps, whom they called in when the rest of them, even his adored dad, failed.

"Just what's the problem there?" he asked, trying not to let these thoughts show in his face.

"The people of Estrella are not colonists from Terra or any of the colonized planets," the admiral explained slowly. "They are native to that world—the first such, by the way, that we have discovered who are advanced enough to be asked to join the Federation with equal status. They are quite man-like in shape, and of a high order of civilization. Their culture is much like Earth's was two hundred and fifty or three hundred years ago."

"Just beginning their real introduction to scientific and mechanical technologies on a planetary scale, eh?"

"That's it. Their system was discovered and mapped a few years ago. The Colonial Board immediately sent psychologists and linguists there to learn their language and study the natives and their form of government, their economics and general advancement. What they found, although far different from our own, was so surprisingly high that we sent them a formal offer to join the Federation. But..." He stopped, frowning.

"Yes?" Hanlon was interested now, and paying close attention. "But what?"

"That's what we don't know. At first they seemed very pleased with the offer. They studied it carefully and, at our suggestion, sent a picked group of statesmen, scientists and merchants on a trip to our various worlds in one of our ships. These men and women seemed delighted with what they found, and enthusiastic about their world joining us. But shortly after their return home and before the final treaties were signed, opposition began to develop."

"What kind of...?"

"All kinds. Enough to make the plans slow down and halt. The embassy sent there couldn't discover the reason—we have trouble enough understanding their way of thinking at all—and they yelled for help. We sent a couple of SS men there, and when they failed, I went there myself, to help them, and the embassy come home."

He shook his head. "I can't find a thing, either, that seems significant. Oh the surface opposition is easily discernable. Papers, handbills, inflammatory speeches by spellbinders, whispering campaigns, all calling for keeping Estrella for the Estrellans and running out all foreigners bent on plundering the planet for their own enrichment—that sort of thing."

"Maybe some natives who want to take over, themselves," Hanlon ventured.

"Could be. We've thought of that, but have found no proof. We have no proof of anything except the opposition. Only one thing, that mayor may not have something to do with this. We've discovered that almost simultaneously with this opposition an unprecedented crime wave started there—every type of criminal activity imaginable, and that is almost unheard of on that world. But we can't even get the first leads as to *who* is behind it all. That's why I suggested you be called in, and the staff agreed."

The admiral paused and his piercing gray eyes bored earnestly into the blue ones of his son. "Keep this in mind at all times, Spence, for it is most important. We *must* succeed there. This is the first non-Terran world we've found equal in cultural advancement to ours. But surely it won't be the last. And we must win them over. All civilized worlds must band together for mutual growth and wellbeing. So this is our most important project just now."

"Yes, I can see that. Also, that if we do get them to join us, we can point out that fact to any other planets we may discover and try to bring into the Federation in the future."

And lying at ease on a heavily padded bench before the control board of a space cruiser, a stranger looked deeply into a multiphased scanner that worked on scientific principles not yet discovered by humans.

For long, long months its mind had been studying this new world and its inhabitants. The language had been learned, after a fashion, as had much of the planetary economics and governmental intricacies. Now the minds of the people were being studied; it was searching, always searching, for certain types.

But part of that mind remained continually in that of one certain Estrellan it had long ago selected.

CHAPTER TWO

SO NOW SSM GEORGE HANLON WAS HERE ON this planet they called Estrella, trying to see what he could find out. It was hard, devilishly and maddeningly hard, to discern what these people were really thinking. It wasn't their language—that had been fairly easy to sleep-learn from the reels. No, it was their mental processes—the way they thought. He was not too sure of himself yet, even with his ability to read their surface thoughts, for so often those thoughts held connotations he was not sure he understood.

For the Estrellan mind was so different from those of humans—its texture was coarser, for one thing, and the thought-concept symbols largely non-understandable to him so far. He had studied—he winced to think how hard he had studied—and he had practiced assiduously since arriving here. But he still could get only an occasional thought-idea of whose meaning he felt at all sure…it was far worse than with humans. True, he was making some progress, but it was so—he grinned mirthlessly—"fast like a turtle." Yet he did not allow discouragement to keep him from continuing with his work.

For during the week he had been here he had managed to pick up some facts of which he felt sure. He decided his best method of approach lay with this new criminal element, for he was convinced from his study of the problem that they were, somehow, tied in with whoever was behind all the opposition to Estrella's joining the Federation of Planets. The tremendous increase in crime, so foreign to the general nature of these high-principled beings, and coming simultaneously with the development of that opposition, was not, he felt sure, coincidental. Working from the inside against a criminal gang had worked on Simonides—it might be equally successful here.

He had found what he felt was proof that a certain Ino Yandor, this world's greatest purveyor of entertainment, was actually a ringleader in the criminal web, in this city, at least. And he had figured that the best way to get acquainted with this man was to pose as an entertainer.

Because of his ability to control the minds and muscles of animals, he decided to be an animal trainer. Hence his apparently strange action in buying eight Estrellan roches, or dogs. He had figured out an act that he thought was a dilly.

"At least," he grinned to himself, "it would knock 'em in the aisles on Terra or the human planets. But with these folks…" he shrugged away the doubts.

Suddenly, as Hanlon was sitting there thinking all these things, he heard a tremendous commotion outside the house. There were the excited yells of many children, a terrific uproar of yelps and whines that he recognized as made by his roches, and the shrill complainings of the elders living in this and the adjacent houses.

"Oh, oh, my pups are being delivered," Hanlon grinned, and ran out to meet the messenger. As soon as he was in sight of the crowd, he began touching one rochian mind after another, sending them calming thoughts, and quieting their frenzied yelpings. By the time the eight dogs were in his rooms, they were well under control, and lay down as soon as they were inside.

Hanlon good-naturedly answered many of the questions hurled at him by the inquisitive youngsters; assured the apprehensive neighbors that he would see to it that the roches did not bother them; dismissed the man who had delivered the animals, with thanks and a gold penta, then hurriedly closed the door against the crowd still in the hallway.

He then settled down into a comfortable seat, and proceeded to get acquainted with his new pets. He first had to learn the texture of their individual minds, which were like yet different from those of earthly animals. Then each roch's individual characteristics had to be studied and learned, and the animal's wild nature more or less tamed and subdued, which last he found quite easy to do—from within.

The animals, in turn, had to become used to Hanlon's taking control of their minds and bodily functions, and of allowing him to handle them mentally without fighting back or trying not to obey.

This was eminently tricky work, but Hanlon's previous practice with many animals, birds and insects, both here and on Simonides and Algon, had given him facility so he was able to do it fairly easily.

"Why, they're really just nice little pooches at heart, in spite of that snout that looks like a pig's, set in that flat face. But I like 'em, and I think this'll work out okay." He fed and watered his pseudo-dogs, then let them go to sleep, as he was preparing to do.

Right after he and the roches had breakfasted the next morning, he set to work in earnest on their training for the special routines he had planned. As the day sped swiftly by he found his ideas working out even more satisfactorily than he had hoped. It would not be too long before he was ready to make contact with that Ino Yandor, the theatrical agent.

The following day Hanlon stayed in his room again, working with the animals, training them in group maneuvers, having learned how to handle them individually. It was a weird feeling, dissociating part of his mind and placing it in that of a roch, and with that portion of his mind consciously controlling the animal's brain to direct its nerves and muscles to do what he wanted done. And when he did this to eight roches simultaneously—well, even though he had done similar things before, it was still hard to get used to the idea that it was possible.

So hard had he been working that he was surprised when he happened to notice how dark it was getting. He went over and looked out of the window in his room, and saw it was night outside. A glance at the Estrellan time-teller on the wall, and he saw it was the dinner hour.

He rose and stretched, yawning vigorously. "Better get out and get some fresh air," he thought. He took the dogs for a half-hour's run outside, then brought them back, fed and watered them. He impressed on their minds that when they were finished they were to go to sleep. Then again he left the building.

He couldn't help grinning a bit as he was walking down the street, thinking of the screwy way these people handled the problem of where to live. For the common, ordinary, not-too-rich people, there were apartment buildings, such as the one in which he lived, owned and operated by the government. When anyone wanted a room or an apartment, he merely hunted around in the district in which he wished to live until he found an empty place that suited him, then moved in. There was no landlord, no rent. Taxes paid for it.

You were supposed to take care of your own cleaning and minor repairs or any special decorating you wanted done. Major repairs were handled upon request, by men paid by the government. If your furniture wore out, or no longer suited you, you simply moved to a place you liked better—and some other poorer person had to take what you had left, if all other rooms were occupied. Yet so considerate of others were the average Estrellans that they seldom did this, preferring to replace the worn-out things themselves, if financially able to do so.

"Imagine the average Terran doing that," Hanlon had thought, wonderingly, when he first heard of it.

He had been lucky enough to find a three-room apartment fairly close to the downtown section of the city, yet far enough away so the crowd noise did not bother him. The building in which he lived was of four stories, and he was on the second floor, near the back.

It was the third place he had looked at when he first come to Estrella. He could not at first make himself believe that all the rooms had such bad smells in them. But he soon found it to be true, largely because these natives had nothing that could be called efficient plumbing. When he had finally picked these rooms, he spent a full day airing them out, cleaning them thoroughly, and using what disinfectants and smell-eradicators he was able to find and buy in the stalls here.

The peculiar looking, five-sided rooms were comfortably furnished, by Estrellan standards, and not too bad even from Earthly ones. The walls and ceilings and floors were painted in fairly harmonious colors, and there was a sort of half-matting, half-carpet rug on the floors. What corresponded to the living room contained two of their low, backless stools, and one quite comfortable lounging chair. There was a large and a small table, and an empty case where one could store any reading scrolls he might possess.

The bedroom had a low, foot-high, five-sided bed, but it was hard and uncomfortable until Hanlon figured how to make it softer, and more to his liking. There were several pegs on the wall from which to hang his clothing, two more of the backless stools, and the open place—a sort of well running from roof to basement—that was the toilet. Hanlon found a large piece of heavy cloth something like canvas, in one of the stalls, and made a hanging to cover this in lieu of a door, which shut out some of the smell source.

The kitchen had shelves, a stove, and table and backless stools. In one corner, suspended through the ceiling, was an open water pipe with a sort of concrete drain beneath. This was both the source of water for cooking or drinking, and the bathing place—a primitive shower.

The reels furnished by Survey had told Hanlon that few of the Estrellan buildings were more than five stories high. "Some, in the business districts, may run to six or seven stories. We have concluded that the main reason for this is that the natives do not have elevators, except a few crude rope-and-pulley freight elevators in some of the stores and office buildings."

Now Hanlon sauntered slowly along the street, enjoying the fresh night air, warmed to about sixty-five degrees Fahrenheit, while he worked the kinks out of his tension-wearied body. This business of controlling the roches demanded such intense concentration that his mind and body were highly keyed up when he finished, and he had trouble relaxing.

He saw, almost without noticing this time, the primitive street lighting system that made flickering lights and shadows on the tree-shaded walks and roads. These people used natural gas for their nighttime outdoor illuminating—just semi-ornate standards with the flames rising a foot or so above them. Men went around at dusk to light them, and again at dawn to turn them off.

Hanlon had walked slowly for several blocks when he saw a native approaching him. When they came abreast the man stopped him.

"I do not remember seeing you about here before," he said, looking closely at Hanlon in the flickering light. "I am the peace keeper for this district," he added as he saw Hanlon's questioning look.

"No. I just moved in a few days ago," Hanlon answered.

"What do you do here? Do you have a job?"

"He thinks I'm a vag." Hanlon grinned to himself, and said aloud, in a courteous voice, "I just came from the Eastern Continent, nyer, and hope to become a public entertainer. I have enough money to support myself until I can earn more."

"That is good. If I can ever be of service in helping you to get acquainted, please look me up. I like to see all the people in my district happy and busy."

"I shall do that, nyer, and thank you for your courtesy." And as the man moved to one side, Hanlon gave him a cheery half-salute, and went on his way. "Darned nice people, really," he said to himself. "They'll make good Federation citizens."

When Hanlon had started out on this stroll he had had no special destination—was merely out for a breather. But as he ambled along a thought came to him, and he quickened his pace and walked more purposefully toward the downtown section and a certain building he had previously spotted.

It was a small "place where men drank," and his investigations had convinced him that many of this city's criminal element went there for relaxation. The cafe occupied the street floor of a small two-storied building that was, as were almost all the Estrellan buildings, a five-sided one.

For *five* was the sacred number of the native religion and philosophy. Hanlon had learned that the number five was consistently used wherever possible, even in their architecture, their ornaments, and their coined money.

Their religion was based on five basic Truths taught by He Who Died For Them. These were: Love, Faith, Brotherliness, Honor, and Loyalty. Their philosophy (they called it their "Code of Living") was also composed of five parts: to be religious; to attain the highest possible mentality; to live physically clean lives; to be considerate of others always, and to be honest in all dealings.

The Terrans had found that while, of course, there were individuals who did not subscribe either to their religion or their

Code of Living, that on the whole the race held a very high standard of ethics.

Now, as he walked inside the drinking place, the young SS man saw that the pentagonal room was brilliantly lighted, rather than kept dim as were most Terran and Simonidean cafes.

"Probably because they can't turn 'em low," he thought. For the lights were lamps burning a carbide compound that gave out a harsh but very bright light.

As Hanlon took a seat at a small table, he looked about him interestedly. There was a bar across the back or third side, where the drinks were mixed. On the other four sides, except where the windows or doors interfered, were several small booths, with drawn curtains across their entrances for privacy. The balance of the floor was filled with two, three, and five-place pentagonal tables, and their chairs, or rather, backless stools.

"What is your wish?" an attendant came to Hanlon's table.

"Glass of mykkyl, please."

While the waiter was bringing the barely intoxicating but very popular drink, and later as Hanlon was slowly sipping it, the SS man let his mind roam throughout the small room, touching mind after mind, seeking and hoping to find those he had come here trying to locate.

He had to grit his teeth to keep from showing the frustration he felt on this world when trying to understand what these people were thinking. For he had long since found that, whatever a human might be speaking in words, his thoughts showed his true feelings simultaneously with and despite what he was saying. And Hanlon could usually read those surface thoughts and understand them fully.

But with the Estrellans, he had found this was not always true. There was sometimes an...an obliqueness...that could not be directly translated by one no more used to their thought-patterns than he was so far.

George Hanlon was the only member of the Inter-Stellar Corps' secret service who could read minds at all—one of the very few humans ever to possess this ability to any demonstrable extent. And he was still young enough to feel occasionally that he was being badly treated by his inability to read these native minds at will.

While he was on that Simonidean assignment, and on the planet of Algon, he had even learned to telepath with the natives, the Guddu "Greenies," or plant-men. But here he could not do that at all. He could read and control animal minds, "and these lousy Estrellans are almost animals," he had growled beneath his breath at first, "so why can't I handle their minds?"

But even through this rude shock to his vanity he did not entirely lose his ability to think and reason logically. He had studied the problem intensively for these past days, and had come to certain preliminary conclusions.

"It's not, after all, that they're lower in the evolutionary scale than we Terrans are," he finally concluded. "It's just that they haven't advanced as far in scientific and technological knowledge. They may look like apes, but they sure aren't. Probably, when we get to really know them—if we ever do— we'll find they are way ahead of us in many things. They certainly, as a whole, practice their 'Code of Living' far better than most of our people do their professed religion."

This conclusion was another shock to his confident young mind. For he had more than half expected, when he first came here, to have an easy time of it in solving the problem on which he and the other secret servicemen were working.

Yet how quickly he had been disabused.

And now, in this little place where men drank, he was finding it out anew. None of the minds he was scanning with all the ability he possessed, was quite of the calibre he sought, although most of them displayed leanings toward larceny and other criminal tendencies. For this drinking place was not one which the more generally law abiding and decent people of Stearra cared to patronize.

Maddeningly meager were the thoughts he could interpret, but when he finally came to scan the minds of four natives who were seated at a five-place table near the back, close to the bar, he made an almost unconscious exclamation of surprise and delight.

He "listened in" more closely to the four, who were leaning toward each other, talking together in low, earnest tones. Hanlon could read the surface thoughts in each mind, but only occasionally at first could he understand what they were discussing. However, as he became more accustomed to their individual peculiarities of thought, he began to get enough to convince him that these were the ones he was seeking. At least, they were planning some deviltries, and one spoke as though he had received orders as to what they were to do.

Hanlon even finally got their names, although of the latter he soon became interested mainly in that of the slender, blondishly-hairy native with the steely blue eyes. That one, Ran Auldin, was their leader, Hanlon decided.

More intently now, Hanlon studied their minds, paying no further attention to the others in the room. He lingered over his drinks for nearly an hour, "listening in" on the conversation of these mobsters, and learning quite a bit about their criminal activities, and better how to interpret their thoughts.

Suddenly he stiffened in even closer attention.

"The leader," Auldin was saying to his henchmen, but Hanlon knew from his side thoughts that the fellow meant Ino Yandor, "wants us to start a series of fires and wreckings about the city. We'll get a list of places tomorrow or next day, and that night we'll do the job."

"In the name of Zappa, why?" one of the men asked. "Why would he want us to do that?"

"Who cares why?" Auldin shrugged. "The leader, he tells us 'do this', and we do it, that's all."

"Sure," another chimed in. "We get paid for our work, and good pay, too. So let the big fellows worry about why they want certain things done."

"That's the way to look at it," Auldin said. "We'll meet here tomorrow evening, and I'll probably have the list. If not tomorrow, then next day. But meet here tomorrow, anyway."

So, Hanlon thought swiftly. Just like small-time crooks everywhere. Somebody with brains does the bossing, and they stupidly follow orders, interested only in the pay they receive, caring nothing about who or what gets hurt.

These fellows were certainly worth watching, he decided. Even if it did not lead him to the larger goal he was seeking—and he felt sure it would—he would spike their plans somehow.

He felt he had heard enough for the time being, so he rose and left the drinking place before they should notice him. He walked slowly back to his apartment, thinking about this new plan, wondering, as the mobster had done, why such orders were given. It made no sense to him, unless it was that the chief criminals were merely intent on spreading a reign of terror and destruction.

"Or are they," he thought suddenly, "planning later to make it seem as though we Terrans are doing it? Perhaps planning to start a whispering campaign of such rumors?"

More than ever now he was determined that such activities must be stopped. "We've got to clean up this planet, and get it into the Federation. If they keep on this way, they can be a real menace. But with this criminal activity wiped out, and Estrella a member of the Federation, we can help them so much—and they have a lot to teach us, too."

CHAPTER THREE

THE FOLLOWING DAY HANLON CONTINUED working with his roches. He now "drilled" them as soldiers are drilled. He taught himself how to control their minds in unison, making them march in all the various complicated maneuvers of squads and columns, all in perfect alignment and cadence.

It was tricky, delicate work, requiring as it did placing a portion of his mind in each roch's brain, giving that mind and body individual commands, yet keeping enough central control in his own mind so they all performed exactly together.

So much of his mind was transferred to theirs, that he had to learn how to make his own body "stand at attention" during these maneuvers, with but minimum control over his own functions.

Hour after hour he worked with them, giving them fifteen minutes of rest out of each half-hour—and thus giving his own brain rest at the same time. For this was tiring work for him, as well as for them.

When dusk fell he stopped the training, saw to it that the roches were well fed and watered, then put them all to sleep. He dressed for the street, went out and found an eating place, where he did full justice to a good meal.

"One thing you've got to hand these folks," he thought thankfully, "they certainly can cook, even though some of their dishes have a most unusual taste."

It had taken him several days to discover which native dishes he liked and could digest, for some of them almost made him ill, others had a taste he could not stomach, but most of them were delicious—and Hanlon was ordinarily a good trencherman.

His meal finished, Hanlon paid and went back to the drinking place where he sat, toying with a glass of mykkyl while waiting for Auldin and the others to appear.

They came in shortly, one by one, and Hanlon "listened in" on Auldin's mind as the chief mobster gave his fellows directions as to the places they were to burn or wreck. Hanlon had already prepared a note, addressed to the head of the local peacekeepers. To this he now added the addresses Auldin was giving. When he was sure he had them all, he slipped out of the little cafe.

He went swiftly along the streets toward the Stearra police headquarters, which he had previously located, keeping watch until he saw a dog-like roch running along. Quickly reaching out and taking control of its mind, Hanlon made the animal follow him until he could duck into a deserted doorway.

Hanlon made his messenger take the prepared note carefully in its mouth, then trot down the street and into the "police station." There it ran up to the man in charge, and raised itself up with its front paws on the man's knees.

"What in the name of…?" The official looked down, eyes bugging and mouth slack at the beast's unexpected action. For several moments he seemed not even to notice the paper in the roch's mouth. When he did, he took it gingerly, opened and read it.

"An attempt will be made just before half-night," Hanlon had written, "to set fire to or wreck the following places of business. If you watch carefully, you can catch the criminals in the act, and save these pieces of property from damage or destruction." Then followed the five addresses.

The man read the note twice, a puzzled, anxious frown on his face. He did not quite know what to make of it—or so his attitude seemed to indicate. There had been no "crime" on this planet that he had ever had occasion to try to stop. For he was not a police officer in the ordinary sense. The Estrellan "peace keepers" merely watched to see that crowds or individuals did not get too boisterous, aided in handling crowds at large gatherings, or assisted home those who may have imbibed too freely.

The fellow scratched the back of his head while he considered the matter at length. "Some phidi trying to make a fool of me," he finally said aloud, as Hanlon heard through his roch's ears, as he had been watching through its eyes. "But how in the name of Zappa did whoever it was train this roch to bring me the note like this?"

This latter problem seemed to have greater interest for him than the warning. For his eyes were still watching the roch with puzzled inquiry…but he did nothing about acting upon Hanlon's suggestion.

As the SS man watched the roch leave the peacekeeper's headquarters, he fumed because it was apparent that the official was going to take no action on his warning. Were they in on this criminal activity, he wondered? Was it that widespread, that even the supposed law-keepers were party to it?

No, he finally decided, probably this fellow was just a dumb, unimaginative sort of dope.

He watched miserably as the fires were set and the business buildings wrecked. There was nothing else he could do to stop it, for he knew it would only put himself in useless danger to try—would jeopardize what he and the other secret servicemen were trying to accomplish here. But as soon as the damage had been done he found another roch, and sent it back to headquarters with another scathing note.

"You paid no attention to my previous warning, and as a result two of the buildings I told you about have been set on fire, the windows smashed on another, and two others have been wrecked by explosions. Why don't you use what small brains you possess, and stop this wave of crime? Or are you being paid to ignore it?"

Through the eyes of the roch Hanlon watched the official read the note, and saw him fly into a rage and pace the floor...but what the man was thinking Hanlon was too far away to read.

"One thing sure, I'll have to get busy and make contact with these gangsters," Hanlon thought bitterly as he went back to his room and to bed. "Guess I'm near enough ready to tackle Yandor now. Let's see, shall I do it directly, or...?"

He undressed and climbed into the low, foot-high, five-sided bed these Estrellans used. There was no mattress or springs, but fortunately his rooms had several extra blankets, and these he had folded beneath him to make his sleeping more comfortable.

He was still wrestling with his problem when he finally dropped off to sleep.

But the next day he figured it out to his satisfaction. He worked with his roches until evening, then went out and got himself a meal. Later he went, purposefully late, into the drinking place. Seeing Auldin and his men already at their table, he went directly up to them.

"Greetings, Ran Auldin," he said boldly. "I've been looking for you, for I want to join your group. I'm fast and clever with knife or flame gun, and I've got plenty of ideas. I can do us both a lot of good."

The other three half-rose, staring at him with hostile eyes. But their chief made a gesture that said, "Wait." Then he looked Hanlon up and down coolly. "You are mistaken, my friend," he said at last. "We are not engaged in such activities as might require the use of…of knife or gun. We are lawful businessmen."

Hanlon fitted his face to a crooked smile and his voice was almost sarcastic as he replied, "Sure, sure, I know. But listen, friend. A fellow out to make a big pile of pentas doesn't do it by being asleep. I've done a lot of scouting 'round and asking questions in a discreet way. I know who I'm talking to."

His mind, always in touch with that of the others, read in their surface thoughts the surprised, "Oh, so that's why we've had the feeling the past few days we were being watched." He could tell that this conclusion made them jittery, and more cautious and ready for instant action.

But Hanlon had to keep on the path he had taken.

Aloud, Auldin merely said again, in a voice he kept mild and low, "I'm sorry, my friend, but you are still mistaken. We work for another man, helping him hunt out talented people and make entertainers out of them."

"During the day, yes," Hanlon gave him a wise smile, "and I can help him a lot in that, too."

He knew the three other men had been growing more and more angry at his interruption. He could interpret their thoughts well enough so he was tensed for quick action, determined not to be caught off guard.

"But what I'm really interested in," Hanlon continued, "is your evening activities. By the way, I hope none of you got hurt or burned last…" He wheeled swiftly, for one of the natives had suddenly leaped up and toward him, a dagger in his hand, slashing at him.

Hanlon met him with a light, contemptuous laugh. He ducked beneath the other's knife slash, then stepped in close.

His left fist traveled only a few inches, but all the strength of his powerful shoulder and arm muscles was in the blow. His fist sank to the wrist in the man's solar plexus.

Wind *whooshing* out, the gangster doubled up in pain. Hanlon chopped down with the edge of his hand on the other's wrist, and the knife clattered to the floor. The Corpsman swung viciously with a right uppercut that lifted his attacker and drove him backward. He crashed into a chair with such force that as man and stool fell to the floor, the wooden seat was splintered.

The other two leaped to their feet and started forward. As though he had eyes in the back of his head and had seen them coming, Hanlon swiveled toward them, his lips thinned in a fighting grin, while several of the cafe attendants were running up.

"Leave him alone," Ran Auldin commanded sharply, and his men looked back at him in astonishment. "The stranger was only defending himself against an unprovoked attack by Ugen," Auldin explained to the cafe's men. He turned to his fellows. "You two take Ugen home and put him to bed. I want to talk to this stranger."

As the surly guards picked up the limp body of their fallen companion and bore him out, the drink servers returned to their posts. Evidently Ran Auldin was known and respected here. He now faced Hanlon and motioned toward one of the stools.

"Sit down, my friend," he said courteously. "Perhaps we can do a bit of talking."

"No use for knives, eh?" Hanlon grinned as he sat down. But immediately he sobered. "I figured maybe you'd be willing to talk, although I didn't expect to have to slap down one of your boys to make you. I'm sorry if I hurt him."

And Hanlon was sincere in this. He had momentarily forgotten that he was on a lighter planet, with a gravity only about 90% that of Terra, and that consequently he would naturally be stronger than the average Estrellan native. While this would not have kept him from defending himself from that sudden, vicious attack, he would have pulled his punches a bit had he thought. He did not like killing or injuring people.

But Auldin was answering, and Hanlon knew he had better be on his toes and pay strict attention. There were undertones and concepts behind the spoken words that were hard for his Terran mind to interpret.

"You needn't be sorry," Auldin assured him. "Ugen was useful, in a way, but he's stupid. I don't especially like stupid people." He studied Hanlon closely. "I don't think you're stupid."

"I don't know it all, by any means," the SS man said with disarming candor, "but I never considered myself simple."

"Now, what makes you think we are engaged in any-thing...illegal...during our evenings?"

"Look, nyer, let's not you and me chase ourselves around a flowertree. If I'm out of line, say so and I'll take a run. But since we're talking here together, all peaceful-like, and there's nobody within hearing distance if we talk low, let's put it on the penta, shall we, huh?"

Ran Auldin looked at Hanlon another moment, his face and thoughts showing puzzlement at the stranger's choice of words. Then he laughed quietly. "By Zappa, I like you, my friend. What's your name?"

"Gor Anlo."

"You're a cool one, all right. Where are you from? I've not seen you around Stearra before."

"No. I'm from Lura, over on the Eastern Continent. The goody-goodies are mostly in charge there, and there's no way for a hustler to make a fast pile. So I came here, hoping there'd be more chances for me. I've been here six or seven days, looking over the ground, and making a little investigation. The best leads pointed to your boss, Ino Yandor."

Auldin started at that name, and while he was staring anew at Hanlon, the latter's mind flashed back over that investigation. His first day had been spent getting the "feel" of the city through wide-open mental searchings. Not so much from individuals at first, but from the mass thoughts of the many. He had later touched hundreds of minds and studied them, trying to learn how to interpret those alien thoughts. He had no trouble getting the thoughts themselves—it was what they meant that puzzled and troubled him.

Now, having noted the start Auldin made at mention of Ino Yandor's name, and the close, searching look the mobster bent toward him, Hanlon continued quickly with an appearance of great intensity and seriousness. "I figured that I could get to him easier through one of his seconds in command, and picked on you."

"One of his...?" Auldin started to ask, then quickly changed his mind. "Because you thought I was more weak-minded?" There was now a hint of anger in the cold eyes.

"Not on your life, Ran Auldin. Because I figured, after studying the set-up, that you were about ready to take over in his place one of these days, probably soon, and that would put me closer to the real power...and the big money."

"Hmmm, I see." Auldin was silent for some time, digesting all this in his mind. He was pleased at the compliment, but somewhat startled at two pieces of information Hanlon had so carelessly tossed out. One, that apparently Auldin was not Yandor's chief or only "second in command" and, two, that this stranger had so quickly and easily divined his secret ambition.

Hanlon, reading his mind, could discern and understand all this. Also, he knew when Auldin began trying to figure out whether this newcomer was legitimately on the make, or whether he was a spy sent by someone—perhaps even Yandor—to check up on him. That last statement of Hanlon's really upset him more than the first, which he had sometimes suspected. He worried about the latter now. It was the truth, all right, but he had not thought anyone else knew it or even suspected it. Did Yandor suspect it? If so, Auldin knew he was in for trouble...bad trouble.

Hanlon decided it was time for him to do a little steering. "Look, Auldin," he interrupted the other's somewhat frightened thinking. "Why not take me to Yandor and introduce me? Let him decide whether he wants to let me in or not?"

For a long moment Auldin stared again at Hanlon, but when he finally answered there was a note of relief in his voice he tried to conceal. Yet he was not entirely convinced that this might not be all part of an espionage trick formed in the fertile but hellishly devious mind of his superior, Ino Yandor. But Auldin was one who preferred to meet his dangers face to face…when they could not be avoided.

"That might not be a bad idea," he said as calmly as he could. "But look, my friend. Don't try to play me for an easy fool. I'd do things about it if you did."

"Sure, I know that," Hanlon's voice was bland and ingenuous. "I'm not figuring on your job—being a yunner I know I've got to begin low and work up. A chance to get started is all I want…for now."

Auldin rose, took some of the five-sided silver pentas from his pocket and dropped them on the table. "Fair enough. Come on."

The two were mostly silent as they walked along the narrow, unpaved, crooked streets, past the not-too-tall, five-sided buildings of the mercantile establishments of this district. After a few blocks of the winding, twisted streets they turned down a tree-shaded residential street. Hanlon wondered, "don't these folks ever learn anything about surveying?" They walked past increasingly pretentious houses, which Hanlon knew were of the ubiquitous pentagonal construction so general on this planet. It was this unusual type of buildings that Hanlon found it hard to adjust to. The first day or two on this planet and in this city the odd shapes and crooked streets had so distracted him he had trouble concentrating on his job.

Now he looked interestedly at the almost-universal green-tiled roofs and also at the gardens of beautiful but strangely unearthly flowers. He saw, too, the thick-trunked, low but wide-spreading flowertrees that lined the streets and were heavily planted in most of the yards surrounding the houses.

He tried, naturally, to see if these latter had any minds he could touch—ever since knowing those plant-like Guddus this had become almost automatic with him at sight of any new kind of tree, bush or plant. But he drew a blank here, as he had elsewhere. Those alien growths on Algon might be unique in the universe, he thought.

Hanlon was glad of Auldin's silence as they walked along. It enabled him to get his own thoughts in order, and to try to plan as best he could for this coming interview with Yandor, not knowing what to expect...except that it would undoubtedly try his abilities to the utmost.

There were some slight traces of fear in his mind, for he was, after all, still a very young and inexperienced man playing a dangerous game. But the thought of his success in his first assignment—the dangers he had faced and the victories he had wrested because of his unusual and growing wild talent— brought back his self-confidence and with it an almost contemptuous view of the dangers here. There was really nothing to fear after all, he told himself. But still...

Hanlon and Auldin came to a place in the street where it climbed a fairly steep hill—there were many such throughout this city—and were nearly winded when they finally reached the top. Still wordless, they were both glad of the chance to stop and rest a moment. Then they started on again, along a much nicer part of the street, rapidly approaching the home of Ino Yandor.

This entertainment entrepreneur (that was, in effect, the nearest approach to a familiar profession of which Hanlon could think) was the one the young secret serviceman's investigations had led him to believe was the first rung on the ladder he must climb to find the knowledge that lay at the top.

"Ah, here's the place," Auldin said at last, as they turned up a sort of cobbled walk leading to the fairly imposing residence. It was an ornately decorated, two-story house, pentagonal in shape, and with a green-tiled roof, of course. The three sides Hanlon could see were painted in different, though mutually complementary colors. The surrounding lawns were made of the peculiar grass so general here, with its minutely petalled flower-tips. There were also numerous beds of the strange, native flowers, highly perfumed, but not heavily blossomed except in the mass.

Hanlon thought he caught large numbers of thought-emanations from animal minds of various kinds, but before he could investigate, Auldin spoke.

"One word of warning. Don't be too eager. Yandor may seem slow thinking and calculating, but don't make the mistake of thinking him stupid. And don't irritate him—he seldom shows his temper, but he is deadly vindictive to those he takes a dislike to. But he is a good employer—and generous to those who serve him well and efficiently."

"Thanks for the tip. I'll be on my good behavior." But Hanlon grinned to himself as he read the reason for that warning in Auldin's mind. If this stranger was spying for Yandor, he would have to make a good report on Auldin.

Then, as the mobster used the ornate knocker, Hanlon tensed himself for—literally—anything.

CHAPTER FOUR

AFTER A CONSIDERABLE WAIT THE DOOR WAS opened. By the light from inside George Hanlon saw a fairly tall native, his hair and beard sleek and burnished from much brushing, and trimmed with unusual care. He was wearing a sort of slip-on gown of heavy cloth, probably a lounging robe. Perhaps the man had already gone to bed—in which case he would undoubtedly be quite provoked at their untimely call, Hanlon thought. Indeed, the man's face showed surprise and petulance at this interruption.

But Hanlon could see shrewdness and a crafty trickiness inherent in the black eyes that caused an inward tremor. "I'd sure better be on my toes with this fellow," he thought.

Yandor scanned the two for a long moment, without a word, then beckoned them inside. But as soon as the door was shut—and locked—he turned angrily on Auldin.

"Well now, what's the big idea, you stupid idiot, of coming here, and at night, and bringing someone with you. Are you trying to cross me, Ran? You know that isn't healthy."

Ran Auldin cringed somewhat and made his voice apologetic. "It's because it was night, nyer, and we wouldn't be noticed, that I came now. Besides, I think this is important. I want you to meet Gor Anlo, who's just come from Lura, looking for a chance, he says, to get into our businesses."

Auldin slightly emphasized that last word, and Yandor's eyes snapped wide. He swung about and faced Hanlon, studying him carefully. The young man bore the scrutiny without flinching, a smile of greeting on his face, but without a sign of boldness or brashness.

After a moment Yandor motioned them into an adjoining room, and himself went to sit behind a large, ornate, wooden table desk. "Sit," he waved a delicate hand at the two chairs facing him in such a manner that the desk lamp's light was strong in the faces of the two, while leaving his own more or less in the shadows. Hanlon could barely repress a grin at this—it smacked so intimately of the old Terran police-questioning technique.

During the short moments they had been in the hallway, however, Hanlon had noticed a small roch standing there, apparently one that Yandor must have partially tamed and kept as a pet. Quickly the SS man had transferred a part of his mind into that of the beast. Now, while his own body and nine-tenths of his mind were in that office room for the interview with Ino Yandor, the other tenth, inside the brain of the roch, was making the animal roam the house, seeking whatever secrets it might find there.

The impresario looked at Hanlon searchingly. "Well now, so you think you'd like to get into the entertainment business, eh?" he said with an attempt at joviality.

"Yes, nyer, that…and other things," Hanlon answered calmly. "Back in Lura where I come from, sir, the people seem to be against the idea of a young fellow getting ahead in the world. So…" He shrugged. "…I came here where I thought there was a better chance of doing myself some good. Me, I'm out after a basketful of gold pentas…and not too particular how I get 'em," he added levelly, but in his eyes was an unmistakable message the Estrellan could not help reading correctly.

"But there are entertainment procurers on the Eastern Continent," Yandor was sparring for time to evaluate this situation better. "If you have a good way of pleasing the people, they would be glad to take you in hand."

"Anlo isn't stupid, Yandor," Auldin interrupted…and Hanlon was glad he did at just that moment. For the roch had just peered through the half-open doorway of a room upstairs, and found a man, probably a servant, lying there on the bed, apparently reading from a scroll.

Hanlon did not especially like this spying on anyone, but he *had* to learn all he could about what was going on here, no matter how he gained the information.

So he reached out and studied the man's mind. The fellow was not reading at the moment, he found, but was thinking of the "payback" he owed someone named Ovil Esbor, who had obtained this position for him. This Esbor was much like a Terran ward boss—a minor politician, but connected with many shady dealings. Hanlon had not previously heard that name, but made a mental note to investigate the man further. He might be another lead.

The SS man withdrew his mind after a bit, and sent the roch searching the other rooms. He noticed quite a few animal pets about the house, but thought nothing special of it at the moment. Meanwhile he, in his own person, began paying more attention to what Auldin and Yandor were saying.

"…been in town several days, he says, looking over the situation. How he found out I don't know, but he knows all our businesses."

Yandor barely repressed a start of surprise, and his crafty black eyes narrowed. "Why are you spying on...no, *who* are you spying on us *for?*" he demanded in cold tones that again sent a shiver down Hanlon's spine. For there was no mercy or lack of ruthlessness in that tone. Nor in the man's attitude. Yet, at the same time, the young man realized stunningly that Yandor, too, was as much afraid of *his* superior as Auldin was of Yandor...and Hanlon knew after a fleet scanning of the gangster's mind that he now felt relief that Yandor had not been investigating him through Hanlon.

But the young SS man had been reading the impresario's thoughts as best he could, as well as hearing what he was saying. He felt that he knew now how to handle this agent.

"As Auldin said, I'm not stupid, and I am on the make for my fortune. I knew the only way was to check first and talk later. So I asked seemingly innocuous questions here and there—and I'm wise enough never to ask more than one from any one person. That way I found out a lot. I do know something about the entertainment business and can hold up my end of the performance. But I also know the really big money is in the other things you control."

Yandor did gasp at that. His face grew black and he half-rose and opened his mouth to say something—but Hanlon beat him to it.

"Incidentally," he lowered his voice but still kept it penetrant as he leaned forward confidentially, "there's someone in the next room, listening through that door there, to what we're saying."

At Hanlon's quiet words, Ino Yandor's eyes opened wide, while Ran Auldin barely repressed an exclamation. Neither guessed, of course, that the stranger was looking through the eyes of Yandor's pet roch which, in the course of its investigation of the house for Hanlon's benefit, had come to the open doorway of that adjoining room, and had seen the man kneeling there, his ear pressed against the door panels, listening intently.

Now Yandor reached into a sort of pigeonhole in his table-desk and quietly took out a flamegun. Tensing himself, he suddenly swung his chair about and leaped to the door. Flinging it open he found, indeed, another man there, before that other could rise and run.

Grabbing the spy's collar with one surprisingly strong hand, Yandor yanked him to his feet and into the light.

"Ondo!" he exclaimed. "Well now, what in the name of Zappa were you doing?"

The small man cringed. "Pardon, nyer, I was…was only trying to make sure that no one was attempting to harm you…and…and standing by to help you if they were."

"I think he's lying," Hanlon said, knowing from his quick probe into the other's mind that he was. "I'll bet he's a spy for someone."

This last, he knew however, was not correct. Ondo was regularly employed by Yandor as a houseman. But he was one of those intensely curious and inquisitive people who always try to find out everything that goes on in any house they happen to be working in.

"By Zappa, you'll never spy again," Yandor's face grew livid. "You know better'n to cross me. You know it isn't healthy."

And before anyone could guess what he was about to do, the raging impresario chopped down with the butt of his flamer, and Ondo fell unconscious to the floor, blood welling from a gash in his forehead. The furious entrepreneur was swinging the weapon into firing position to kill the fallen man when Hanlon leaped forward and grasped his arm, holding him back.

"Wait, nyer. Don't cinder him," he said almost in a tone of command. "It wouldn't look well for a man of your public position, if word of it ever leaked out."

"I say kill the snake," Ran Auldin spat. "There's no sense taking chances with a man we know is a spy."

"No!" Hanlon was still quietly determined to save Ondo's life. He spoke as impressively as he could. "Such a killing, with a body to dispose of, would most certainly be traced back to you in time, nyer, and you would lose much of the respect the public holds for you. Your success in your...other...endeavors is largely due to the fact that everyone knows you for such a high-principled, public-spirited citizen, that no one suspects you of being anything else. Don't take chances on spoiling that reputation."

Yandor was swayed by this impassioned appeal; it was plain to be seen. His respect for Hanlon's quick good sense and sound judgment mounted, and he looked at the young man with new interest.

"Anlo's right, Ran," he told his lieutenant. "We mustn't have a killing on our hands that can be so easily traced to us."

He turned back to Hanlon, who was grinning inwardly at Yandor's almost-panic that made him forget for the moment that there were no real police detectives on this world who could so easily trace back a killing, especially if only ordinary precautions were used to dispose of the body.

"Well now, I thank you for saving me from the risk my temper might have caused. What would you suggest we do with this...this...?" He pushed at the body with his foot.

"It's easy to see that Ondo is only a scared rat, and when he wakes up he'll know he'd better keep away from you or he'll really be killed," Hanlon spoke carelessly. "Just have Auldin take him out and dump him on the next street. Ondo will never bother you again. I'm positive."

Auldin seemed about to protest, but Yandor forestalled him. "That's good advice. Take care of it, Auldin."

And after the gangster had left the house with his burden, Yandor resumed his seat and motioned Hanlon to take the one he had formerly occupied. But while they were doing this, the young SS man had sent his mind outdoors, found a sleeping bird and taken over its mind. He made it follow Auldin, so he would know where Ondo's body was taken. He would try to save the fellow's life if he could—he had got him into this predicament, it was up to him to get the chap safely out of it.

"Well now," Yandor was saying, "I'm beginning to believe you will be a valuable man in our group. I'll think about it some more, and see you sometime tomorrow and we'll talk further about it. But I'm only promising to talk," he added hurriedly. "I'm not saying what my decision will be."

"That's all I could ask for now, for I know I can prove my worth." He rose and bowed courteously. "So I'll see you at your place of business in the morning."

"You know where it is?" he said surprisedly.

"But of course."

As soon as he was out of the house, Hanlon went carefully to the weed-infested vacant lot where Auldin had dumped Ondo's body. When he saw the gangster returning, Hanlon quickly hid behind a great flowertree.

Hanlon had brought the bird back to Yandor's house, and now made it perch where it could look through a window. Through the bird's eyes he saw the two inside, talking together for some minutes—Yandor apparently very angry, Auldin on the defensive. Then the slender mobster slunk from the house, and started back toward the downtown section. Hanlon made the bird follow him, to make sure Auldin was really going home, and was not circling about to try to find out what Hanlon was doing or where he was going.

Then the SS man went to the vacant lot to find Ondo sitting up, holding his aching head. Almost roughly he jerked him to his feet.

"Look, you phidi…" Hanlon made his voice deadly menacing. "…I don't like people who go around trying to find out about me and my business. Yandor merely insisted that I see to it that you left town immediately, but I'm not that soft hearted. I'm going to kill you, then I'll know you've done your last snooping."

He reached toward his pocket, as though for a knife or flamegun.

The man was a small, terror-stricken rat. But he was not entirely lacking in the universal will to live. Suddenly he half-stooped, then jumped forward, his shoulder crashing into Hanlon's body. The young Corpsman could have maintained his balance, but he let himself fall, as though he had been knocked down by the blow.

Ondo took off like a scared dara, and in brief seconds was out of sight. Hanlon waited several minutes, then went down the street toward his rooming house, grinning to himself. He was happy that it could be worked out this way.

He was sure this Ondo would leave Stearra without delay. Hanlon's hint about that was enough, he was sure—especially since he knew Ondo was convinced that he would be killed out of hand if he ever allowed himself to be seen hereabouts again.

As he walked swiftly along, Hanlon released the bird from its mental spell, for it was now apparent Auldin was really going downtown, or home. But before releasing the bird, Hanlon guided it back to a comfortable perch in a tree, and put it to sleep.

He could not help feeling gratitude—yet still with an awed sense of wonder—about his ability to control animal minds. He remembered so vividly that day on the great spaceliner *Hellene*, when he had discovered this tremendous ability with the little puppy...what was its name...? Oh yes...Gypsy. And the still greater thrill when he was experimenting later with the dogs on the kennel deck, and had found that he could not only read their complete minds and control their nerves and muscles to make them follow his bidding, but that he could also dissociate a portion of his mind, put it in their brains and leave it there, connected with the balance of his own mind merely by a slender thread of consciousness, yet able to think and act independently.

But it certainly came in mighty handy in his work as a secret serviceman, and he was thankful to whatever powers may be that had given him this ability to do these amazing things. Now if he could only learn how to read and control the whole mind and body of a human, instead of being able to read only their surface thoughts!

But he was trying to learn to be content with what he had, and to use it thankfully.

Yet he never ceased trying to learn more—to be able to do more along these lines.

Finally back in his room Hanlon grinned again to himself as he began undressing. He felt good. He had put it over again. He was sure he was "in."

He sat down on a chair and removed the special shoes he was wearing. These native Estrellans were very manlike in shape as well as mentality, but there were enough structural differences so it had taken the expert cosmetician many hours to fix him up to look like one of them. These shoes, for instance, because Estrellans had unusually large feet, were really shoes-within-shoes, to fit his feet correctly inside and yet appear large enough on the outside not to attract attention.

In the spaceship high above, intent thoughts had been coursing through the mind of the being. Finally, certain commands were impressed upon the mind of the Estrellan native the being controlled, that would set in motion a new train of events.

The native cringed as those thoughts came into his mind. They were not the kind of things he would ever consider, of himself. They outraged his every sense of right and justice. It made him actually, physically sick even to contemplate them, and he wondered briefly how he had ever come to get such ideas.

Yet something, he could not guess what, forced him to do them, despite his every struggling, heartsick effort not to obey the commands he did not even know were commands.

CHAPTER FIVE

AS SSM GEORGE HANLON CONTINUED undressing, he recalled his parting with his father on Simonides.

"How soon do I start?" he had asked, boyishly eager, at the close of their interview. "Right away?"

"Whoa, son, not so fast," the admiral laughed. "You'll have to have a series of inoculation shots against the Estrellan diseases. Then you'll have to learn a lot, and especially, you'll have to be disguised to look like a native, which isn't easy. Here are reels of the language, customs and geography. Get a room in the hotel here and sleep-learn them. I think you'll find the language not too hard—it's a simple, uncomplicated one, outside of their habit of putting the verbs ahead of the nouns, and then the adjectives or adverbs. As to their way of thought—well, that's far different. Even with your ability to read their minds, I'll bet you have trouble in really understanding them for some time. I'm not always sure I do, even yet."

"Tough, eh?"

"That they are. You can't work them like you do humans—their concepts seem not at all like ours in so many things. We can get in serious trouble through misunderstanding their apparently straightforward words. So go slow and easy."

"I'll watch for that, dad, and bone up on the rest as fast as I can. Meanwhile, how's about going out and wrapping ourselves around a couple of thick steaks—or some of that good *poyka* at the Golden Web? I'd like to see Hooper again."

"The grub I'll buy. But Curt isn't here—he's one of the boys working Estrella with me."

The lessons learned in time, Hanlon visiphoned Admiral Hawarden at Base, who sent the cosmetician to him at the hotel. The shoes had been only part of the job. There was the smock-coat, which Hanlon was now removing in his room in Stearra. Estrellans had narrow, sloping shoulders, so a tailor had made special clothes—the coat almost like a knee-length, slip over sweater only of a heavy cloth like homespun, with shoulders whose cut and padding gave them the proper sloping look. There was also the divided-skirt sort of pantaloons, which gathered at the ankle.

As he undressed Hanlon looked at himself in the mirror, and grinned. Trevor had dyed his skin all over—not the dark red of Terran Indians, not yet the black of Negroes nor the brown of

Malayans, but a sort of deep pink. Hanlon had been warned not to take either tub or shower baths, but had been supplied with a bottle of a special chemical.

Naked at last, he scratched luxuriously and stretched hugely. He poured a bowl full of water, added seven drops of the chemical, then gave himself a sponge bath.

As he was washing his face he noticed with amusement the way his ears had been built up with plastic to almost twice their natural size, and the way his nose had been made so much broader—like a giant ape's it spread over half the width of his face.

He was careful not to pull off any of the hair that had been so painstakingly glued to his body to simulate the general hairiness of the Estrellans. And, of course, he had neither shaved nor had a haircut since being assigned this job and his beard was growing nicely. But it, and the body hair, was the most uncomfortable part of his imposture—the darned stuff itched, but bad. He scratched.

Anyway, he thought thankfully, Trevor had really done a job on him. No one yet met here had seemed to notice anything out of the way with him, as far as his looks went. He had easily passed everywhere as a real native.

A two-man speedster had brought him to this planet, and had landed him just outside this city they called Stearra, in the dead of night. His father, he knew, had preceded him by nearly two weeks, was here somewhere, as were Manning and Hooper, the two other SS men assigned here. A sneak boat came every two weeks, and stayed at a designated spot near the principal city on each continent from midnight until three in the morning, in case any of the men wanted to send messages or needed assistance of any kind.

Undressed—and scratched—and washed—and scratched— Hanlon lay down on his bed and gave himself up to thoughts of the coming interview at Ino Yandor's office. He tried to analyze what he had learned and its possible connection with whatever it was that was keeping Estrella from joining the Federation of

Planets; from becoming the fifty-eighth member of that far-flung union of self-governing worlds.

It seemed to him he had made a good start—although he was slightly dissatisfied with the speed at which he was not getting ahead. Yet he had felt all along—and still so thought—that with his way of working his best course lay through the criminal gangs of Stearra—that by working up through them he would eventually come to the ones who were behind all this. And he was sure this Ino Yandor was his best lead to date, even though it seemed strange that an entertainment agent would be the top man in the criminal world.

His father had not been too certain that this was a logical channel of investigation, but was quite willing to let Hanlon try it—the Corps had to have that information, and each man of the secret service should work the way that seemed best to him. Nor could the admiral argue against Hanlon's insistence that this sudden rise of hitherto-unknown criminal activity just at this time was not purely coincidental.

But the whole thing was such a seemingly insoluble puzzle. From his own investigation since he had arrived—from the "feel" of the city and its inhabitants to his sensitive perceptions—Hanlon knew the people on the whole were such swell folks; the kind that would make wonderful Federation citizens, even if they did look so peculiar and animal-like to Terrans. Any race with a religion and a code of living based on such common decencies and high-principled honesties as theirs was bound to be a good one.

From all he had been able to learn, Hanlon thought the Ruler, Elus Amir, a decent fellow and extremely capable. Amir certainly had shown by his actions all during his tenure of office that while their system of government was a sort of limited autocracy, that he, at least, was trying to make it a benevolent one. Unless all the information Hanlon and the SS had gathered was haywire, this Amir was certainly not behind all this sudden opposition. He had seemed—especially at first—to be very much in favor of joining.

Then who in the name of Snyder was?

Suddenly a new idea brought Hanlon upright on the bed. Was Amir merely a tool—like the emperor of Sime had been under Bohr? Was there someone here who was comparable to that devilish Highness? Somebody with Bohr's brains and driving lust for power and ever more power?

Hanlon sucked in his breath in sudden wonder—and worry. Was this unknown another alien from the same, or some other advanced and faraway planet as yet unknown to the Corps, working to take over Estrella and possibly—or finally—the rest of the Federated Planets and the whole galaxy?

It took Hanlon a long time to go to sleep...nor had he found the answers to his puzzle when he finally did drop off.

*　　*　　*

When George Hanlon appeared in Ino Yandor's office just before midday, the dapper impresario ushered his visitor into an inner room and closed the door.

"I think Ondo has left town—or died. For I have heard nothing more of him, nor have any of my men. You were right about a killing that could be traced to me being bad for my carefully built reputation. Well now, about your working for me. You said you knew something about the entertainment business. What can you do?"

"Well I can't sing or posture, and I'm not much good at acrobatics. I can whistle a little, and..."

"'Blow'? What is that?" Yandor used his definition of the word Hanlon had translated as meaning "whistle."

Oh, oh. Hanlon knew he had blundered. In an effort to cover up he said, "This," and puckered up his lips and whistled a few discordant notes, concealing the fact that he was an excellent whistler, and could do perfectly dozens of birdcall imitations.

"No. I'm afraid that is nothing our people would care for."

"Then how about an animal act?"

This was the crucial point. Hanlon had given a lot of thought to this and had worked out the idea he thought might apply here. It certainly would go big back on Terra, he knew, but he was not yet conversant enough with Estrellan theatrical acts—even though he had gone to the theatre several times to study them—to know if these strange people would like it or not. But he had to get in the good graces of Yandor.

"What sort of an animal act do you have in mind?" the impresario asked doubtfully. "Our audiences are very particular. It has to be good, very good, and unusual."

"I think they'll like mine," confidently. "I have eight pet roches, and as…"

"Roches!" Yandor looked incredulous. "You mean you've actually trained some roches?"

"That's right. I've trained them as a hobby. I drill 'em just like our Ruler's residence guards do—and other things as well. I'm sure the people will like the act. I'll bring 'em down and show you what they can do."

"Well now," still hesitantly, "that may be all right. It sounds most unusual, to say the least. I'll look at them, say, the day after tomorrow—yes, I think I'll have time then."

"Thank you, nyer. Then, after I've shown you what I can do about that, we can talk about…other things."

There was a flash of anger in the snapping, black eyes. "Don't press me, Anlo. I go slow about things like this, and I'll want to know all about you first."

"Sure, I know that. I didn't mean to hurry you—I just wanted to remind you I was still thinking about the main thing, not merely about a little matter like being an animal trainer."

He left the offices then, and started toward home. But on the way he began thinking about that man, Ovil Esbor, he had heard mentioned. He took a couple of hours out, then, to investigate many minds to see what he could learn about the fellow.

He found that his initial information was correct—Esbor was a small-time, local politician, but was also connected with many other businesses about the city. He ran a sort of employment agency as his business "front," but there were rumors that he was also a "fence" for stolen goods, a panderer and narcotics agent, and many other illegal things.

These latter, however, Hanlon registered in his mind as merely rumors, not facts, for he could get no direct evidence of them, even though he "read" about such things in many minds. But he was convinced that the man was one about whom he should learn a lot more, as he had time for such investigation. He felt sure that Esbor fitted in somewhere in the chain of criminals Hanlon was so sure was tied in with the group who were trying to keep Estrella out of the Federation.

He went back to his apartment then, and to the training of his roches. He was well satisfied with them—he liked them as pets, and they had learned to like him. When he first came in they swarmed all over him, and all of them had a good romp before he got them down to serious business.

He was also quite happy about the way things were going. He was putting it over again, for he felt certain that through Yandor he could get the dope he needed on the higher-ups. Yandor had never even so much as denied that he had other irons in the fire than his theatrical business. And from vague ideas Hanlon had seen in the man's mind from time to time, he felt surer than ever that he was on the right track.

That evening he again went out for some fresh air. As he was strolling aimlessly down the street he saw an elderly Estrellan native approaching. The fellow seemed very friendly, wanting to stop and chat—and Hanlon found himself grinning inwardly at the old man's garrulous good nature, so like that of Terran elders, something he had not before found here.

The young SS man touched the other's mind almost as a matter of course at the outset, and discovered that the man had lived in Stearra all his life, but was now a lonesome old widower, all his family and friends gone on before him or moved away. Here was a good chance, Hanlon thought, both to be nice to an oldster and to get some more general and perhaps specific information.

"Will you do me the honor to have a drink with me, nyer?" he asked courteously the first time the old chap gave him an opening. "There is a very nice place where men drink close by."

"That's mighty kind of you, yunner, mighty kind. Don't many people act that way to me anymore. But there was a time…" His voice trailed off, but Hanlon read in his thoughts of the days when the fellow was an important and popular man in this city.

As they walked along the street to the drinking place, Hanlon listened with half an ear to the old fellow's chatter, while he was thinking swiftly. It had not taken him long to learn that in this secret service business he had to take information wherever, and from whomever, it was to be gained. And this old geezer ought to be quite a mine of gossip. Hanlon hoped he could steer it into channels of real information.

Once seated at a small table, and their glasses of mykkyl before them, Hanlon broke into the monologue to say engagingly, "I've been in Stearra such a short time, nyer that I don't know much about it. And since I intend to make it my home from now on, I want to know all I can about things and people here."

"Heh, heh…you came to the right place for that, yunner. Where you from?"

"I was born in Lura, over on the Eastern Continent. But I found there was not much chance for a young fellow to make his fortune over there—everything is owned by a few rich people who keep all the businesses in their own families. So I came here."

"Yes, you did right. There are plenty of chances for bright young fellows to make fortunes here in Stearra. Hey ah, I remember well…" And the old fellow started in on what Hanlon knew would be a long, uninteresting resume of his past life. So he interrupted with a question, or rather, a request.

"Please tell me who are the most important people here, and what you know about them."

For nearly an hour he kept the old fellow on this topic, in spite of the innumerable lapses when the man started wandering in his reminiscences.

Once, when Hanlon had ventured to ask directly about Yandor, he learned a very interesting fact that he gave considerable thought to when he was back in his own room. This was the fact that the impresario was crazy about animal pets.

"He has what almost amounts to a menagerie at his home," the old fellow cackled. "Always on the lookout for new and unusual types and kinds. Why, they say he even has cages outdoors, containing lots of wild animals—even has them brought to him from the East Continent and the polar regions."

Hanlon remembered now, that when he first went to Yandor's house he had seemed to sense many animal minds near him, but had not taken the time to investigate. Also, that the roch had shown him quite an unusual number of pets about the house.

So, after Hanlon had bid the old man good night, the young SS man settled himself in his most comfortable seat to consider this angle, as well as the other things he had learned that night.

Actually, while great in quantity they had been meager in quality, telling him little that he desired to know. The oldster had not known anything about any organized opposition to Estrella's joining the Federation nor, more particularly, who was behind it. Oh he could repeat glibly much of the propaganda that was making the rounds, and which Hanlon already knew. How, if Estrella joined the Terran planets it would lose its own planetary sovereignty, and become merely a minor cog in the great schemes of the people led by Terra, who were out to grab the whole galaxy for their own ends of power and greed. That Estrella's people would have to conform to human standards rather than their own, and that their splendid Estrellan culture would soon be entirely lost. That they would end up by being little more than slaves.

"Why," he cried with genuine dismay and anger at one point, "it is those Terrans who are doing all the criminal things that have been making life here so dangerous recently—all those robberies, fires, murders, and so on, that our people would never even dream of doing."

"Where'd you hear that?" Hanlon queried sharply, aghast that his surmise should thus quickly prove correct.

"Why, everyone knows that; everyone's talking about it," there was surprise at his question. "You mean you didn't know it?

"But it's true. That's the sort Terrans are. They don't even consider us real people," he added indignantly, almost crying in his drink. "They actually think we are inferior to them—that we are just semi-intelligent animals. Hey ah, how stupid can they get? They should know we Estrellans are the highest form of life in the whole universe!"

Hanlon knew this vicious propaganda was false, of course. He wanted to tell the oldster about how they actually worked with the primitive but intelligent races of other planets—what he, himself, had helped plan for the Guddus. But, of course, he could not.

He could have told this old man that while the Corps and the Federation statesmen recognized that the Estrellans were not as far advanced in some sciences and technologies as were the Terrans and their colonists on other worlds, they did respect these people as possessors of excellent minds and abilities. That they readily acknowledged that the Estrellans were far ahead of them in ethics and in ways of living together peacefully.

He could have added that these statesmen knew, and stated, that if the Estrellans wanted to learn the sciences and techniques the Federationists possessed, they could assimilate that knowledge in a very short time. But, also, that the Federation would never try to *force* their knowledge or culture on the Estrellans or any other peoples. That they never tried to make any of the less educated or less-advanced beings of other worlds conform to any mold those people, themselves, did not desire and specifically request be taught them.

But at the moment this other thought interested Hanlon more than a political review. So Yandor liked pets, did he? Well, how better get in his good graces than give him one never seen on Estrella before? Hanlon would get him a brand new animal, one far different from those on this planet, where all the native animals were tailless.

Yes, and it would be one with a brain that could give Hanlon a real chance to see and hear what was going on in the man's private life when Hanlon could not be near him.

"Let's see now, when's that sneakboat due…hey, it's tomorrow night. That's great. I'll be there to meet it."

CHAPTER SIX

IT WAS NEARING DAWN ON THE EASTERN *Continent of Estrella, and high above in the stratosphere, in its spaceship, the strange being that had been studying this planet so carefully, suddenly stiffened to closer attention. Its mind had just contacted a group of beings below whose minds were of a far different texture—finer, somehow—than those of the natives of this world. The language was different, too, which did not make so much difference. But the thought processes of these newcomers, in many cases, were almost incomprehensible to the alien.*

What were they? Was there more than one race here on this planet, after all? The being activated its multiphased scanners, and studied and pondered.

SSM George Hanlon was waiting in the shadows of the great forest enclosing the hidden clearing when the spacer came in. When it had landed, the lock-door opened. Hanlon ran over and, after giving the correct password, was helped inside the ship.

"Hi, fellows," he greeted the two secret servicemen who were assigned as crew of this ship, and went with them into the control room. "How's everything in the great big universe outside of this dump?"

"Not bad," they grinned. "Nothing special going on. Mars just won the interplanet baseball championship..."

"...and there's a new singer on stereo that's a doll, boy, a doll..."

"We saw Hoop and Manny at our stop on the other side, and they said the admiral was coming here. We got some letters for him, but you'd better take 'em in case he doesn't show before we have to leave."

"Okay, will do. Hey, you fellows got any candy bars? Can't get sweets here, and I'm sugar starved."

"Sure, plenty." And while one of the men went to the storeroom, the other asked Hanlon if he would like a cup of coffee.

"Gee, I sure would. That's another thing these folks don't have. That herb tea of theirs...ugh!"

The first returned with a dozen candy bars that Hanlon stuffed in his pocket, and continued drinking his coffee.

"Oh yes, better give me some Estrellan money. I've had to spend quite a bit recently. About five hundred credit's worth should be enough." They gave him that from a supply in a drawer.

"Now for the most important thing," Hanlon said. "Next trip I want you to bring me a cat—a nice black..."

"A cat?" It was a duet of surprise.

"Yeh, a nice, tame, housebroken Earth cat. All black, or maybe with a white star in its forehead. About a year old, and quite large. Be sure it has nice, sleek fur."

"Can do, all right," doubtfully, "but for John's sake, why?"

"One of the men I'm working on here loves pets and collects all the different kinds he can get. So I want to give him something he doesn't have. All the animals here are tailless, so get me one with a really nice, long, well-furred tail. A thoroughbred, not an alley cat. I figure it will help me get in good with him."

"Right." One of them made a note. "Anything else?"

"Not a thing, thanks. 'Specially for the coffee and candy. Wonder when da...the admiral will get here?" He hoped they had not noticed that near-slip, for it had been decided the relationship should not be generally told, and so far only a few SS men and high officials knew of it.

"Haven't the faintest."

"Then I guess I'll stick around awhile and see, if you don't mind."

"Glad to have you aboard, mister. We have to stay here several hours anyway, and we like company. Getting sick of old Tom's ugly face anyway," one of them quipped.

"Yeh, I 'spose you think you're a beauty queen."

"You play poker?"

"Lead me to it."

Though Hanlon carefully avoided using his special mental abilities, when Admiral Newton came aboard an hour or so later, the young Corpsman was a few credits ahead. The cards had just fallen right for him.

After the two secret servicemen had left the cruiser and it had blasted off, they started back toward town. Hanlon had very much wanted to see his father, for he had been vaguely disturbed and dissatisfied with his rate of progress. True, he was making a good start at getting where he wanted to go, but it seemed to him he was taking far too much time for what little he had accomplished. He said as much to his father.

"Well I don't know," the admiral said thoughtfully, as they rode along the flowertree-shaded but dusty road. "These things take time, and it seems to me you haven't done so badly, considering the short time you've been here."

"Thanks for being generous, but I seem to be taking so long for next to nothing."

"What do you plan to do now?" Newton asked, and Hanlon explained more in detail what he was after.

"What makes you so sure this fellow Yandor leads to the higher ups?" the admiral asked slowly at last.

"All the clues I've managed to pick up so far point to him as a key figure," Hanlon said earnestly. "I've read in a number of minds facts—or snatches—that point to him as one of the leaders, despite his reputable position as the leading theatrical entrepreneur…"

"Or because of it," his father interjected.

"Yes, perhaps because of it. When Auldin introduced us and I hinted at my knowledge of his 'other activities' and when I've mentioned them since, Yandor didn't react as I'm sure he would if he wasn't engaged in something off-color."

"Hmmm, it all sounds reasonable. And as far as the time that it's taking you is concerned, you needn't worry yet. It always takes time to open up a line of investigation. You took three months or more off to go to Algon, remember, but you got the answers finally."

They had arrived at the house where Hanlon lived so they parked their trikes in the back yard, and went up to his room.

"Yes, what you say is true," Hanlon seemed more relieved now. "What have you and the others found out?"

His father's short laugh was not a pleased one. "Hardly a thing worth mentioning. We don't even have any leads that may be successful, as you have. Manning has been working as a clerk in a government office, but can't find a thing. Hooper is in Lumina, the secondary capital where the study and suggestion body holds forth…"

Hanlon's mind remembered from the reels that this body was not exactly a legislature or congress, since it had no power to make laws. It studied all questions and problems that came up, and reported or made suggestions to the Ruler, who had the final say. It was something fairly recent, introduced by Elus Amir.

"…and managed to get a job on an Estrellan equivalent of a newspaper there. But he hasn't found a thing, either, except that he's been in a position to learn where the propaganda is strongest, and is keeping charts and graphs, with dates and percentages, of its spread. But so far they haven't shown anything conclusive, except that the rumors are spreading rapidly, and that lately they have included the whispers that Terrans are back of the crime wave."

"Yeh. I've heard that. Obviously a 'whisper campaign' started by the real conspirators. But what're you doing, dad?"

"Mostly I'm just traveling here and there, keeping as quiet and undercover as possible, trying to find out what people all over the planet are really thinking. The percentage who believe the propaganda seems very small, but is growing. About the only thing I've found out at all curious or extraordinary is that Adwal Irad, the Second-in-Line seems to have a much greater than ordinary place in the counsel and affections of Amir, the Ruler."

Hanlon laughed. "That 'Second-in-Line' business is screwy, isn't it?"

The admiral sat back in his chair, lighted a cigarro, and grew thoughtful. "Yes, from our standpoint it is most peculiar, and one of the things that make it so hard for us to understand the Estrellans at all well. How it is done I haven't been able to find out, but the men of the ruling class are specially bred—reminds me of the way queen bees are developed. They are larger physically, less hairy, and far more brainy than the average males here. However, it seems to sap their strength to handle the job, for while the new ruler takes over at the age of thirty, at the end of his fifteen year term of office he is an old man—yet the average Estrellan life expectancy is ninety." He shook his head.

"Sure is alien all right," the younger SS man furrowed his brow in concentration. "Never heard of anything like it before." He was silent a moment, then looked up. "But what about Irad that's different—I should think the rulers would want their successors to learn as much as possible about the job before they took over."

"I gather they do, but usually in a perfunctory sort of way. However, ever since he came back to Estrella—Irad was one of the natives who went on that personally conducted tour of the Federation—he has been with the ruler almost every day. It is said the old man treats him more like a son than a successor;

they seem, from reports, to be closer even than Amir and his own son."

"Aren't the two related?"

"Not that closely. I believe Irad is a sort of second cousin's son. There's an examination among each generation of ruler possibilities, and the high man is designated 'Second-in-Line' and so on down."

"What d'you 'spose it all means?"

"Have no data yet. It could be something—or nothing."

"I'll keep Irad in mind, then, and watch for a place to fit him in. Oh by the way, how long before he takes over?"

"About two years, I think. Why?"

"Just thought that might be important. I'll hunt around and find out." Hanlon paused a moment, then continued slowly, "but the more you tell me of what you and the boys have not found out, the more certain I am that my way is best—for me, at least—and that I can get some dope through the gangs here."

"I'm willing to buy that now. I'll grant that whoever is back of all this opposition may be, and probably is, using the criminals, and you may get the first leads, at that. In fact, you already have more than we have. But I think we'll find—if we ever learn—that someone far above their level is the prime operator."

"You think there's a possibility it might be some alien—like Bohr was on Simonides?"

His father sat upright and looked at him penetratingly. "I hadn't thought of that." Then he slumped down again. "But I wouldn't say so. It would really be stretching coincidence way out of shape for it to be the same sort of set-up you found there. You haven't found anything to make you think that, have you?"

"No. I don't really suspect anything of the sort—just can't forget how surprised we were back there when we found out about Bohr."

"Well, we'll just have to keep on plugging. The campaign is so obvious—so open with all its use of pamphlets, spreaders of rumor, and the same arguments everywhere...it seems we certainly ought to find some leads somewhere. But..." He shrugged helplessly.

"There's certainly a clever propagandist in the background somewhere. And he sure keeps well hidden."

The elder made a pained grimace. "You can say that again."

"Say...I've got an idea. How about having Hooper or Manning, or bring in still another SS man, to come here and let me brief him on what I've found out about two or three other natives who seem to be up in the gang world? I've got leads on some others who are apparently lesser gang bosses, but I haven't time to follow them up and keep on with my other lines of investigation, even though I think they're important enough to study. Having someone else here to work on them would get rid of a lot of the criminal activity, I'm sure, and would leave me more free to work on Yandor and his superiors. This Yandor is fond of pets, and the sneakboat's bringing me a cat next trip, and through its mind and eyes and ears I can watch him when he's at home, and so on."

His father stared at him in surprise. "A cat...?" Then he shook his head with a helpless movement, but grinned feebly. "You continually amaze me, Spence. I hope it works out."

"Oh I'm sure it will. Yandor makes a hobby of animals, and anything as strange and wonderful—to Estrellans—as a tailed cat he'll undoubtedly keep with him most of the time. Especially after I impress on tabby's mind that it is to love Yandor wholeheartedly, and be very distressed when away from him." He grinned wolfishly...

"Sounds good if you can work it, and I am sure you can. As to the other..." He thought in silence for several minutes, then, "I'll have Manning come here and go to work with you. Being a government clerk, he could pretend he wants to get into local politics, and it'll all seem natural to the natives."

"Fine. One of the locals I suspect is a sort of political boss. I'll brief Morrie on all I know, and suggest some things he can look into to start with."

"And Hooper and I will check more closely into the gangs over on the Eastern Continent," the admiral said. Then he leaned forward earnestly. "We've got to solve this. At first it was merely asking a new world with a high civilization to join us for mutual benefits. But now that this opposition has grown so strong, if we fail here we'll have that much more trouble with other non-Terran worlds we discover. You know Colonial has dozens of survey ships out all the time, and since they cracked that new-type drive of Bohr's, and increased our speed nearly 300%, those exploring trips go both farther and faster."

"We'll get 'em, dad." Hanlon got up as his father rose.

Admiral Newton was still not too optimistic. "I certainly hope so. Well, keep trying, son, and don't get into any more trouble than is necessary."

"I won't, Dad. Safe flights." The admiral left.

After his father had gone, Hanlon sat thinking seriously, and trying to make plans. The roches, which he had kept asleep while he and his father were talking, he awakened and fed, then romped with them for a time.

But Hanlon was not really in the mood for play, even though he had come to feel a great affection for these fine animals, and they for him. He had too much on his mind for such recreation just now.

One thing, he suddenly realized—the roches had brought to his mind—he had been forgetting. That was the series of burnings and wreckings that Auldin and his men were continuing nightly. Despite his notes to the local peacekeepers, Hanlon knew they had done nothing to stop these depredations, and it made him angry.

"What sort of dopes are those peacers, anyway?" he growled to himself. "Are they in on all this, too? They must be. And yet I must remember they've never run up against anything like this before and probably haven't sense enough to figure out what to do. So, it's time I did something about it. But how? Should I try the same thing, or something else?"

He slept most of the day, making up for his wakefulness of the previous night. When he awoke he considered his problem. Due to the fact that he would probably be working his roches in public in a few days, and in a way he believed Estrellans had never seen them drilled or trained before, he was afraid that if he sent another note by means of a roch, as he had done before, someone in authority might be clever enough to put two and two together and not get five. So he decided to use an ordinary messenger.

After dinner Hanlon went again to the little cafe that Auldin and his men patronized, but this time he did not go in. Having been in touch with Auldin's mind so many times, he now knew its texture and individual characteristics well. So when the mobster and his men went into the cafe, Hanlon not only knew it but had no trouble "hearing" Auldin give his crew their assignments for that night's dirty work.

He had again prepared a note for the peace officers, and now he added the new addresses to it. Then he went down the street until he found an Estrellan boy, to whom he gave the note, directions and a coin. The boy ran to the peace station and gave the paper to the official there.

"We are giving you one last chance to serve the taxpayers and citizens who support you," the note said. "You paid no attention to the previous warnings, but we are giving you the benefit of the doubt. We believe you simply did not know how to handle such a situation. It is simple—send a number of men to each of the places listed below, and have them hide and watch. Then, when they see the criminals come to start their nefarious work, have them run out and arrest the men, and bring them back to your station. There they can be held for trial, by the Ruler or someone he appoints. Now get busy, or else…"

"Where did you get this?" the official asked the boy after reading the note.

"Some man gave it to me on the street, and gave me a silver penta to bring it to you," the youth answered, then ran out before he could be questioned further.

Three of the gangsters were arrested that night, but somehow—either through his own shrewdness or through someone's blundering—Auldin escaped.

In the spaceship the strange being knew a feeling of profound disquiet. It had followed the two of those strange minds that flew the space-cruiser to its second landing place on this world. It had known when these beings met one and then another additional one of these unknowns who were not like the natives of this world. From the fact that the first two came in a spaceship— which these natives did not possess—the deduction was simple that they were all from some other and unknown—to it—planetary system.

But one of these newest minds could not be touched at all! The scanning intellect knew only that such a mentality was there because the first two (and later, a third) were so evidently holding a long conversation with someone…and in its multiphased scanner the being could see that that someone was apparently an Estrellan native.

Why, then, could not its mind be touched?

In its scanner the two were followed as they returned to the city and to a dwelling place, and one side of their conversation was "listened to." They were clearly, the mind was forced to conclude, a menace to its carefully laid plans.

But why could that one mind not be read?

CHAPTER SEVEN

IN THE MORNING, ALTHOUGH STILL FUMING about Auldin's escape, Hanlon had to put it out of his mind as he prepared for the tryout of his act before Yandor.

The new and gaudy uniforms had been delivered and the roches had grown used to wearing them. Now Hanlon dressed himself and the animals and left the house. They marched down the street toward the downtown section where Yandor's office was located.

Naturally, the procession attracted considerable attention, for Hanlon made the roches follow him sometimes in single file, then close up to double file. They always kept evenly spaced, all in perfectly cadenced step. He, himself, strutted in a sort of drum major's fashion, for he considered all this excellent advertising.

"Wish I had a brass band," he grinned to himself. "Then these folks would really wake up."

By the time he reached the more densely-peopled business section, a large crowd was watching him and his unusually trained and dressed dogs, and comments were lively and pleasantly surprised. As on Terra—or any other planet, for that matter—this parade attracted an ever-growing crowd of excited children, who tagged along with laughter and shouts of joy.

Into Yandor's office Hanlon and his roches marched, and at his brisk command they lined up before the startled entrepreneur's table desk in a double rank of four. "Salute," Hanlon said, and the dogs stood on their hind legs simultaneously, and raised their right forepaws in salute.

"Well now," Yandor gasped, "what have we here?"

But Hanlon, without answering, turned to his roches. "Attention." The roches dropped to all fours, and aligned themselves. In rapid order Hanlon made them do columns right and left, right and left turns, left and right by twos and fours, right and left obliques, and finally right into company front. Then, "Company, halt. Parade, rest."

The roches, who had obeyed every order with precision and unanimity, sank to their haunches and crossed their front feet.

The impresario had stood watching with open mouth and bugging eyes during this miracle of training. Now he rushed up and seized both Hanlon's hands.

"Well now, that's wonderful. Perfect. I've never seen anything like it. Marvelous. Can they do anything else, too?"

"Certainly." Hanlon then explained rapidly the various other things he had trained his roches, individually and as a group, to do.

"Well now, we certainly can use this. The people have never seen anything like it. They'll be enraptured. Let's talk terms."

Hanlon faced the roches, who had not moved. "At rest."

They relaxed and lay down, although still keeping their places. Most of them hung out their tongues and panted in the manner of dog-like animals everywhere. Nor did they move from their places during the half-hour or so Hanlon and Yandor were talking business.

All during that discussion Hanlon carefully watched the mind of the man before him, paying more attention to any stray and extraneous thoughts than he did to their talk about bookings—which actually did not especially interest him. For he had begun to find that in those side thoughts of the natives during a conversation usually lay his greatest mine of information.

Hanlon was becoming more and more certain that this man Yandor had much on his mind besides the entertainment business that was his front. He was not able—yet—to get any direct clues as to who Yandor's superior or superiors might be, but he did glean enough to make him certain there were such higher-ups.

Just as they were closing their interview Hanlon said, "I understand, nyer, that you have quite a collection of rare animals."

"Well now, that's right. I do have quite a number, and am always looking for new and unusual ones."

"Do you happen to have a Terran cat among them?"

"A cat? What is that? I never heard of such an animal."

"Oh but you must have one of those. They are not only the finest pets anyone could possibly have, but they have long, furry tails."

A gleam of interested desire came into Yandor's eyes. "I've heard of animals with tails, on other planets, but I've never even seen one. Well now, such a thing would be most wonderful—a magnificent addition to my collection. But how can I get one?"

"If you'll permit me the pleasure, nyer, I can get one for you. I know a certain man on the Eastern Continent who obtained a pair when he was on that trip to the Terran planets. Lately they have had a litter of kittens, as the young are called. I am sure I can buy one or...or...well, I'll get you one," he grinned.

"Oh I would so like to have one—though I hesitate to let you take such risks. But from you my friend I'll accept it. Well yes, I'll gladly accept it from you. When can I have it?"

"It may take some days, but have it you shall. I'll bring it as soon as I can. Meanwhile, where and when do you want me to perform first?"

"Well now, let me think. The National Theatre would be best, I think. Yes, it is the finest and largest here in the capital, and I'll make a special presentation of your opening. I'll invite all the finest people, including our glorious Ruler and his staff. Yes, three days should be sufficient to arrange it all, if the Ruler is free that evening. Where do you live? I'll send you word."

The next three days were extremely busy ones for Hanlon— and he had little time for spying on the mind of Yandor, save when he saw him briefly. Feeling in a way that he was being derelict in his duty, Hanlon nevertheless decided that to gain the best results later he would have to concentrate for the time being on getting ready for his debut. So much depended on that being a success.

He had attended the so-called theatrical performances—more like variety acts or what he had read that the old-time vaudeville shows were like—since he had decided to make his bid for contact with Yandor by this means. Now he went to the "place of performances" to study the layout more carefully and minutely.

It was nothing like the various types of theatres he had known so well on Terra. For one thing, it was not in a building at all, but merely a specially prepared plot of ground, surrounded by a high stone wall. Naturally, being Estrellan, it was five-sided.

Inside the wall the hard-packed and smoothed ground sloped gently downward from all sides toward a level, tile floored, foot-high place in the center that was the stage. The customers stood during the performance, although Hanlon had never been able to understand why.

"Sure seems as though it would be easy, and not too expensive, to at least give them benches of some sort to sit on," he thought.

Near one corner of the stage was the entrance to a flight of stone steps that led downward into the dressing rooms and property-storage for the theatre. When it was their turn, the actors had to come up these steps and so onto the stage to begin their turn, without benefit of curtain. Also, because of the peculiar construction, it was impossible to use "backdrops" or "sets" as Hanlon knew them.

The morning Hanlon went to investigate the place there was no one around, so he was not stopped nor disturbed while he made a complete tour of the underground rooms, and stepped off the measurements of the stage. One great lack amused him.

"What?" he chuckled, "no popcorn or soft drink dispenser robots?"

He had noticed when attending previous performances, that they used no type of footlights or other illumination whatever, and that it was hard for those in the back of the enclosure to see what was going on down in the center. By judicious inquiry he found that on the nights when it stormed or was cloudy, or when Estrella's two moons were not in the sky, there was no performance.

Following his inspection of the theatre, Hanlon went to the market place again. He hunted out a stall where lamps were sold, and after the usual considerable haggling and dickering, bought twenty of the most powerful of the peculiar carbide lamps at a fairly reasonable price. Then he hunted up a metal worker, and had reflectors made to his order and specifications, and fitted to one side of the lamps.

"I'll introduce 'em to something new," he grinned, then was suddenly worried. "Or are such new customs and innovations taboo on this screwy world?"

Another thought occurred to him the second day, and he hunted around for some time until he found a place where masks were made. The customer, who specialized in things for actors, did not have what Hanlon wanted, but after it had been described, the merchant said it would not be hard to make, and that it could be delivered the next afternoon. So, Hanlon ordered a facemask for himself, that would look like the head of a roch.

Meantime, he continued working with the animals whenever he had time. He was now well satisfied with his ability to control them under all circumstances. He felt sure he would have no trouble in "putting on a good act." And his only worry was whether or not he could please these strange people. For so much depended upon his making good—if he did he would be more solidly in the good graces of the impresario, Yandor. And that was the main thing he was after right now.

The night of Hanlon's first performance finally arrived—and so did a nice large attack of stage fright. There were "butterflies in his stomach" and he was by turns wet with sweat and almost petrified. Peeking out from the top of the stairs leading to the dressing rooms, the sight gave Hanlon a prime case of the jitters. For it seemed all the high officials, business and professional men, and the "social group" of Stearra with their wives and families, were there. Even the Ruler was seated at stage-side in a large, ornate throne-chair, having been persuaded by Yandor that he would see something most exceptional.

Hanlon went slowly dawn into the cubicle assigned him and the roches, and there fought for calmness. And it was a measure of his innate strength of character that he succeeded. The jitters passed, the butterflies went into hibernation, and his nerves calmed dawn.

The first acts were the usual type seen on Estrellan stages—singers, posturers (they did not seem to have any dancers in the sense that Terran theatres do), and acrobats. Hanlon had always been interested in these, for almost none of the things they did were like what he was used to seeing or hearing.

The music, however, he could not get used to. Estrellan music was based on a five-toned scale, of course, and was—to his ears—more of a cacophony than Chinese music. Yet the Estrellan singers had clear, beautiful, flutelike voices.

The footlights that Hanlon had finally persuaded Yandor to have set in place around the edge of the stage, and lighted, occasioned great comment at first. But once the performance started, and the people found how much better they could see, were acclaimed as a great achievement.

"How did you ever happen to think of them?" Yandor had asked when Hanlon first spoke of them and showed the impresario what he had made.

Hanlon shrugged. "I always feel cheated because I can't see better when I go to a performance," he said. "When I got to thinking of my act, I knew it wouldn't show up well if people couldn't see clearly exactly what my roches were doing. So I figured out these lights. Don't you like the idea?"

"Well now, yes, I like them. But I don't know. People are peculiar about change. They may do something about it if they don't approve of them."

"Well," Hanlon made a nonchalant gesture, "we can always turn 'em off if they yell."

But after the first few moments, when the customers had seen how much better they could watch the posturer who came on first, the value of the footlights was clearly seen, and they gave their whole-hearted approval. A new custom was born on Estrella.

Hanlon had been below in the cubicle assigned him and his roches, so had not seen nor heard the crowd's reactions to the acts that preceded him. When it came his turn to go on, he was glad to find that his nervousness was gone, and that he was perfectly calm.

Yandor stopped him near the head of the stairway leading up from underground, while the native who was manager and a sort of master or announcer of acts made a brief speech.

"Nyers and nyas and you, most gracious k'nyer," he addressed the throng and the Ruler, "tonight you are to see something most unusual in trained animals. I have been connected with performances for many, many years, but never have I seen anything to equal this. I will not attempt to tell you what is coming—you must see and marvel and judge for yourselves. Next on our program is Gor Anlo and his Friends."

Hanlon came up the stairway and onto the stage, followed in single line by his eight roches. There was a titter of laughter at first sight of Hanlon in the roch-mask and the dogs in their gaudy uniforms, but this soon quieted in amazed surprise at the exhibition they were witnessing.

Across the entire stage-place the roches marched, while Hanlon took his place in the center. He did not utter aloud a single word of command as the eight roches marched about the platform and stopped in a circle facing the audience on all sides, all the dogs equidistant from the others. As one they rose on their hind legs, and their forepaws bent to their heads in a salute.

A moment they held this, then still without a spoken word of command, dropped to all fours and in rapid succession formed and marched in company front and lines of two and four, made left and right turns, marched across the stage in oblique lines, did about face and to the rear, and all the complicated maneuvers the Ruler's residence guards did on the parade ground.

Then they added some things Hanlon had never seen Estrellan guards do, but which were more or less common to Terran drill teams. They did full wheels in lines of eight and four, formed wheeling stars and circles.

Never once did Hanlon utter a word of command that anyone could hear; never once did the roches falter or break that perfectly-cadenced step; never once was one of them out of line. There was never any hesitation, never any breaking of ranks even when, about halfway through their drill they changed to quick time—almost double the cadence m which they had first drilled.

How could any of that great, stunned audience guess that the trainer was actually controlling each animal mind, that his own mind was divided and parts of it superimposed on each animal brain, so that it was impossible for them to act counter to his central—yet individual—command?

All the audience could see was the most perfect, the most incredibly flawless precision of training they had ever witnessed. Led by the Ruler they began a rhythmic chant of "Yi, yi, yi, yi," in cadence with the roch's marching tempo. The chant grew louder by the moment until it was a deafening roar.

At their first sounds Hanlon almost lost his poise—for he did not know that this was their method of giving highest applause—and that very few acts ever received it at all. He had never heard it when he had attended their performances before. To him, now, it sounded more like they were giving him earthly "boos," and he was afraid he had somehow offended them.

He withdrew part of his mind from each of the roches, even as they were marching across the stage, and sent it out to contact the mind of the Ruler and several others. He was pleasantly surprised at what he read there, for it was not dissatisfaction, but a combined wonder and delight at what they were seeing.

Quickly he again sent full measure of his mind into each of his roches to continue the drill—nor had anyone noticed any break in their routine during the second or so of this mind-searching.

Finally, after a full five minutes of this, Hanlon silently commanded each one, in unison, "Company, halt. Right, dress. Parade, rest. Salute."

He himself came to a stiff salute, his directed at the Ruler. Higher and still louder grew the chanted roar. Even the Ruler sprang to his feet, his sounds of approval nearly as loud and unrestrained as the rest.

When the noise subsided a bit, Hanlon gave the roches "At rest," and they relaxed, lay down, and panted, but each still in his place.

Hanlon stepped forward and facing first one way and then the other said, "Thank you for your kind reception of our poor efforts. Now with your permission, I would like to show you some of the individual abilities of my little friends."

But while he was speaking four of the animals had gone off to the side near the entrance to the stairway. Hanlon had fixed up a specially prepared chair. To the bottoms of each of the legs he had affixed light wooden rods that extended out several inches. Now the four roches each picked up a rod in its teeth and thus lifted the stool, which they brought out and set before Hanlon. He looked down at them in pretended surprise, then out at his audience, and smiled. "My friends are so thoughtful. They must think I am tired and need a rest. Well, far be it from me to disappoint them." And he sat down, while the roches went back to their places and lay down.

Instantly there was a loud, angry hissing from the audience. There was no mistaking this—it was censure, not praise. Hanlon was dumbfounded. What had he done wrong?

Quickly he scanned a number of minds, and found he had broken one of their most sacred taboos. Nobody—but nobody—ever sat in the presence of their beloved Ruler without his express invitation.

"Oops, tilted!" Hanlon groaned, quickly rising and shoving the offending stool off the edge of the stage. But the audience was not mollified. If anything, their clamor rose louder.

It was the Ruler, himself, who quieted them. He rose and held up his hand in a gesture of silence, smiling forgivingly.

"Boy, what a swell egg he is," Hanlon mentally wiped the sweat from his mind's brow. "I still don't understand these folks. I'll have to watch myself more carefully, all the time."

He bowed his thanks to the Ruler, spreading his hands in a gesture of apology. Then he quickly made the roches begin their other tricks. He had one do some acrobatics in imitation of the type their native acrobats did. Two of the others "danced" together. Another balanced himself and rolled about the stage on a large plastic ball Hanlon had secured. Three of them did intricate circlings about each other, without ever getting in each other's way or breaking step at any time. Another stood on its hind legs and "sang" in imitation of the singers. Another "walked" on its front legs. These, being more to the liking of his audience, yet something they had never seen animals do, or so well soon recaptured their interest. After a bit they began again that "Yi, yi" of applause. By the time Hanlon's turn was over the people seemed to have forgotten his one blooper, and were solidly "with him." As he left the stage and went below with his roches, their yells were the loudest yet.

Ino Yandor was wildly enthusiastic, and those who had seen the first night's performance spread the word. In days the fame of Hanlon and his roches had spanned the continent, and other cities were clamoring to see his act while the National Theatre there in Stearra was packed nightly with capacity crowds.

During those days Hanlon spent as much of his time as he could wandering about the city, the marketplace, the recreation parks, and sitting in various places where people ate or drank. With his mind he was hunting not only for whatever points of specific information he might glean, but also to get a more general and better "feel" of the people and conditions here.

He was confirmed in his early beliefs that as a whole these were wonderful people; that they would make excellent citizens of the Federation. They had such a high sense of Social Justice; such deep feelings of right and wrong; such splendid habits of cooperative living. More even than the Terrans and the colonists, who had come far along the road of brotherliness in the past centuries, these Estrellans had an innate belief in the brotherhood of man.

What a great gap there was between the great mass of Estrellans and those few criminals with whom he was working? He remembered one time when he had been talking with his father about the way he worked.

"You want to be mighty careful," Admiral Newton warned. "Being around gangsters and criminals so much, you'll have to watch not to begin thinking like they do."

"You never need worry about that, dad," Hanlon had been very earnest. "The more I see of 'em, the less I like 'em, and the more I'm sure the common decencies of life are best. We must have law, government and order, and all decent citizens must always 'live and let live'. I could never be contented otherwise."

CHAPTER EIGHT

THE NIGHT THE SNEAK BOAT WAS DUE TO return, Hanlon early sent word to Yandor that he was ill, and could not perform that night. The entrepreneur came, boiling over with anger, to Hanlon's rooms.

"Well now," he began, "what's all this about…?"

"Ooh, quiet, please," Hanlon moaned. He had been ready for just some such thing, and was lying in bed, face contorted with pain, and now pressed his hands to his ears as though Yandor's loud voice was more than he could stand. "Can't you see I'm sick? Why must you make so much noise?"

The agent was taken aback by this counter thrust. He calmed a bit then, but asked many questions. Hanlon's partial answers and evident pain finally convinced the impresario that his star performer was, indeed, too ill to appear.

"These attacks come only once or twice a year, and usually last only a day or two," Hanlon assured him in a weak voice. "I'll try my best to be on hand tomorrow."

"Very well. I'll expect you then. Well now, there is something I've been meaning to talk to you about, and now is a good time. I want you to work into your act various things to say against the Terrans; about how such wonderful performances as yours would be impossible if we were to submit to them and accept their so-called invitation to join their Federation. Suggest to the audience that we would all become slaves, and that neither would performers have time to prepare their acts, nor would the others be allowed to come and watch them."

Hanlon was slightly prepared for this because he had seen it forming in Yandor's mind, but he did not like it any the better. He was just about to make an angry retort when he took himself in hand, and continued keeping in the character he had assumed. He groaned a bit louder, and twisted more violently on the bed.

"Please, nyer, leave me now. I hate for anyone to see me while I'm like this. As for what you've just said, we'll talk about it later and see what can be worked out."

And reluctantly it seemed, Yandor finally left.

When night at last brought its cloak of darkness, Hanlon put the roches to sleep and slipped quietly from his room. Down in the back, though, he could not seem to get his tricky acetylene-powered engine to start. He fussed and tinkered for nearly two hours before he could finally get it going.

"So help me, I'm never going to cuss out a real ground-car after this because it acts up occasionally," he said as he rode out of the yard and down the dusty street. He drove as fast as he could out to the clearing where the sneakboat had already landed.

"Sorry to be late, fellows," he said as soon as he had given the password and been allowed aboard. He accepted gratefully the cup of coffee they gave him, and griped for five solid minutes about those gosh-awful excuses for transportation these so-and-so natives used.

"Here, have a box of candy bars, and quit bellyaching," one of them said at last. The other held out another gift, a pound can of pulverized instant coffee.

"Hey, these are wonderful," Hanlon's spirits rose as if by magic. "You guys are my friends for life."

"Why, Georgie," one of them simpered. "I didn't know you cared."

"You'll have to choose between us, though," the other said owlishly. "I'm not going to be a partner to bigamy."

Then they both laughed. "Look, he's blushing."

"Aw, I am not," Hanlon spluttered. "It's just this pink skin dye," he added weakly.

"Anyway, here's your cat," the SS men got down to business, and fetched the crate containing the beautiful animal. "We happened to remember hearing that these people don't have milk, so we got you one that's accustomed to a meat and vegetable diet."

"Gee, thanks for that. I'd completely forgotten that point."

Hanlon examined the big, black cat, and his mind reached out and quieted its fright at the strange surroundings and this hairy being who was now handling it.

He talked with the men for some further time, told them he had not yet got any sure clues, but was beginning to get an "in" with some people he felt sure would lead him to some. They told him the other three men had reported about the same, although Hooper said the curve was rising steadily on the belief that Terrans were behind the crime wave here.

"Yeh. I've heard that bilge, too. It's just another of the things we'll have to stamp out before we can win out here. But we will."

"Sure you will," the two agreed. "Anything else you need?"

"No, can't think of a thing. The cat was the most important for now. It will really get me in more solid with Yandor, the guy I'm working on."

"Hope so, Han. Well, cheerio."

"Safe flights, you guys, and thanks again."

On the ride back he was glad he had a tricycle instead of a two-wheeled bike, for the crate was heavy and rather awkward with the cat in it, shifting its weight about from time to time.

Back in his room once more, Hanlon released the animal, which immediately dived under the bed, where it cowered in fright, having seen and smelled the roches who were sleeping in various places about the rooms.

But again Hanlon reached out and touched its mind, calmed its fear, and soon had it out of hiding and creeping into his arms. It lay there, purring, while he stroked it and impressed on its mind—whose texture he learned while doing this—that it was safe and with friends.

After he had done that, he woke the roches. At first sight of the feline a couple of them started toward it in curiosity. Swiftly Hanlon took over their minds and halted them where they were. He then brought each of them to the realization that this was a new friend and playmate. That was not too hard, for the roches had never seen a cat, and only its strangeness had made them curious.

He had more trouble with the cat, for the ages-old dislike and fear of dogs was strong within it. But he finally calmed it by implanting the knowledge firmly in its mind that these strange beings were not dogs, actually, and that they meant it no harm, and all were to be friends.

Soon he was grinning at his ability, as he saw the nine animals eating, drinking and playing together, as though they had been the best of comrades all their lives.

"I'm really quite an animal trainer," he chuckled to himself as he watched them.

High above the strange being lay on its padded bench and frustrated thoughts ran through its mind. It had noticed the two DIFFERENT minds that again had come briefly to this planet in their ship of space, talked with the three other different ones, and then had come to this western continent in its night time. The mind "heard" them conversing with that other but unreadable mind again, but still no sort of contact could be made. "Why?" it wondered again. What sort of mind was it, that it could not be touched?

Through its multiphased scanner the being carefully watched that entity below which appeared so like an Estrellan native—but after it had left on that peculiar conveyance, bearing a container with a strange animal, sight of the entity had been lost among the crowds of the city streets.

So now the mind above seethed with questions, to which it could find no logical answers, even though it was beginning to understand the thought-concepts of those others it could "read."

Late the next day—for Hanlon had quickly adopted the actors' habit of beginning his day at noon—he fed and watered his animals, then got his own meal and ate it.

Then he impressed on the minds of his roches that they were to behave themselves, and not destroy things about the room in their play, and not to make too much noise.

"Sure is handy to be able to do this," he smiled. "Boy, what a baby sitter I'd make if I could control humans this way."

He called the cat to him, snapped on the harness and leash the SS men had brought with it, and took it down to Yandor's office.

He had worked carefully on the cat's mind, and knew the characteristics and texture thoroughly. He had practiced seeing through its eyes and hearing through its ears under all conditions—from ordinary daylight to bright carbides, from dusk to the blackness of a closet. He felt certain he could use the animal as planned, under any and all conditions.

"This is 'Ebony'," he explained to Yandor as he presented the cat. At the same time he was impressing on the feline's mind that this was to be its new master, that it must always obey him, and must allow itself to be the man's constant pet and companion without hesitation or animosity.

"'Ebony'," Hanlon went on saying to Yandor, "is the Terran word for 'black', and that is probably why its former owner gave it that name."

The impresario took the big, beautiful animal in his arms and exclaimed over and over at its wonderful appearance, its sleek lines, soft fur and intelligent face. But it was the cat's long, furry tail that was his greatest delight. He stroked and petted it as though he could not really believe such a thing was true. Hanlon was careful to explain to Yandor how he must stroke with the lay of the fur, and never *against* it.

"Well now, I can never thank you enough, my friend, for this marvelous gift," Yandor said. "I hope it didn't cost you too much."

Hanlon made himself cough in an embarrassed manner.

"Well…er…it really didn't cost me…" He grinned and left it at that, nor did Yandor, after a knowing look, refer to the matter again.

Instead he said, "It shall be the prize of my collection. I shall treasure this above all others."

Yandor really was in the transports of delight, known only to collectors who have made an unusual find. Hanlon read from the surface of his mind the thought that this man was a wonderful friend, "and probably no menace to our plans at all. I am sure we can trust him—and use him."

The latter phrase delighted Hanlon, although he was careful not to let his feelings show in his face. This was what he was after. He had only to learn who "we" was. But he was making progress; he could really begin to learn things.

"You do not need to keep the harness on Ebony all the time," he explained aloud. "Just when you want to go out with him. In your home or office, leave it off, as it is probably not too comfortable. I'm sure," he decided to do a bit of direct suggesting, "that you'll soon grow to love the cat enough so you'll want to keep it with you all the time. It will lie on your desk, or in your lap, and be the finest sort of companion."

"Yes, and be the envy of all my friends," Yandor swelled with importance.

Hanlon explained rapidly about its feeding and drinking habits, and that while it was housebroken it should be taken outdoors several times a day. When he was sure Yandor knew how to care for the animal, Hanlon left the office and went back to his rooms.

After the performance that night, Hanlon went quickly home and lay down on the bed. He sent out a portion of his mind to contact that of Ebony, which Yandor had taken to his own room and installed in a padded basket, as Hanlon had suggested.

Through the cat's eyes he could see the interior of Yandor's bedroom, and watched while the latter prepared for bed and finally dropped off to sleep. Then Hanlon withdrew his mind, and did the same.

He had set the wakeup on his time-teller for fairly early the next morning. Immediately upon awakening he sent part of his mind back into that of the cat. All during the day—which he spent mainly lying down or sprawled in his easy chair, when he was not preparing or eating his meals, or attending to the wants of his roches—he watched Yandor at his daily activities.

For the impresario, delighted with his new pet, kept the cat with him all the time, even to taking it into the office-like study of his home with him. There, as soon as they were inside, Hanlon made Ebony leap up onto the table-desk, and curl up on the one corner. He wanted this habit to become a permanent one—and it, too, delighted the Estrellan.

Now the cat was in the best possible place for Hanlon's spying while Yandor was at home.

Later in the day, when it was time for the entrepreneur to go to his downtown office, he put into effect another suggestion Hanlon had made. He put the small, ornate harness Hanlon had given him for that purpose onto the cat, snapped the leash to it, and took Ebony with him.

Dozens of Yandor's friends stopped him and complimented him—though somewhat jealously—upon his acquisition, which made him prouder than ever. For Ebony created such a sensation that it took Yandor nearly an hour longer than usual to get to his office.

He had not yet reached there, in fact, when Hanlon was surprised and a little nettled by a knock on his apartment door. Somewhat angrily he got up off the bed, and went and opened it. A native was standing there, grinning.

"What d'you want?" Hanlon growled querulously.

"Boy, are you in a temper this morning?" a voice said in Terran, while the grin grew lopsided.

"Morrie!" Hanlon yelled, throwing his arms about the other. Then, over his shoulder, he noticed a number of his neighbors peering out of their doors, or standing about in the hall, listening, and knew with a sinking feeling that they must have heard the Terran words, and be wondering about them. His mind raced, then he spoke even more loudly in Estrellan.

"My brother, it is such a surprise to see you here. How did you happen to come from Lura to visit me?" Then he dragged the surprised SS man into his room, and shut the door.

"What gives? Why that 'my brother' routine?"

"Noticed the neighbors gawking, and knew they had heard us talking Terran. But I sure am glad to see you, even if I was so curt at first. Was concentrating on a job, and didn't like being interrupted just then."

"Oh, sorry. Want me to come back later?"

"No, no, it wasn't really that important." Hanlon was silent a short moment while he disengaged the part of his mind that was in Ebony, and brought it back into his own. "Come on, take that chair. Go ahead and gab while I get dressed."

Manning did as requested, and they talked seriously for some time, each bringing the other up to date on all they knew about their part of this business, and what they were planning.

In particular, Hanlon told Manning about the local aspect of the work of the criminal elements, and what he suspected as well as what he actually knew and had done.

"I'm almost certain now," he said, "that the criminals and the folks who're trying to keep Estrella out of the Federation are tied in together, but I haven't any real proof...yet. But I think I soon will have, with the line of investigation I'm on."

"We've about come to the same conclusion," Manning said thoughtfully, "but we haven't any more proof than you have, if as much."

Hanlon told him about stopping Auldin's "wrecking crew" and a few other possible leads he had uncovered to local men who seemed to be in on the activities here, especially one Ovil Esbor, a local politician.

"He's a sort of gang boss or district captain," Hanlon added, "but I think he has quite a lot of fingers in different illegal pies."

"I'll get right at it," Manning said. "The admiral—he sent his regards, by the way—said we were to work together as closely as possible, and that you would feed me leads whenever you got 'em—as I will you."

"Sure, I will. Maybe I'm sticking my neck out, trying for the big fellows and asking you to take care of the smaller fry, but it seems..."

"Think nothing of it, little chum," Manning waved his hand airily. "As long as we clean out this hoo-raw's nest, I don't care how we do it, and I'm ready to work at anything. The admiral said—and what you've told me clinches it—that I'd better be an aspirant for a spot in the political setup here, so I'll pretend I heard about Esbor, and go right to him."

For another hour they discussed ways and means, and then Manning rose to go, after telling Hanlon where he was living here in Stearra.

"We'll see each other every few days," he said.

As soon as Manning was gone, Hanlon threw himself on the bed and again sent part of his mind back into that of the cat, now with Yandor in the latter's office. And Hanlon kept it in Ebony's brain all the rest of that day and early evening. But nothing in which he was particularly interested happened—and he was beginning to wonder if his ideas about Yandor were right after all. Nothing but legitimate theatrical business had been transacted all day—at least while Hanlon was watching. There had been those two hours or more while Manning was at his rooms...

During the time Hanlon was on the stage that night, he had to concentrate all his mental faculties on his roches, and had to withdraw from the cat's brain. But once back in his dressing room and while going home and after he got there, Hanlon watched carefully the party the impresario gave to a group of friends in his palatial home.

Through the cat's eyes Hanlon carefully studied each one of the guests and listened avidly to their talk—and at times had to tighten his control of Ebony's mind and muscles to keep it acting friendly toward some of those people. They seemed to "rub its fur the wrong way." And did, literally, on occasions. Also, they had an effluvia Ebony distinctly did not like.

But under Hanlon's compulsion, it continued to act in as friendly a manner as cats usually do...most of the time with customary feline indifference.

CHAPTER NINE

THE NEXT DAY HANLON ALSO SPENT IN THE cat's mind, when he was not playing with or attending to his roches, or eating. It happened that he had transferred part of his mind to each of the eight, and was giving them a short workout, when there was a sudden noise at his door, and it was roughly flung open—he had not locked it while at home.

Nine parts of his mind saw through nine pairs of eyes the man who stormed in. Nine pairs of ears heard him snarl, "What's the big idea of having my men arrested?"

As quickly as he could Hanlon started bringing the portions of his mind from the roches into his own brain. He sat up on the bed, and made his face look blank—but inside he was thunderstruck. How had Ran Auldin found out he was behind those arrests?

"Why...why," he pretended to stammer. "I don't know what you're talking about, Ran. What arrests? What's happened?"

The usually fastidious gang boss was now dirty and his clothing soiled and rumpled. His eyes were red, apparently from sleeplessness, or worry, or both. His voice was still accusing as he answered, "My men were surprised at their work the other night, and I only escaped by luck. Been hiding ever since."

"But what's it all about? Why were they arrested? I don't know anything about what you were doing. Yandor didn't tell..."

"It must have been you. Nobody else knew."

"And I tell you I was not told, either, so how could I know? I've been too busy getting my act ready and putting it on, and Yandor hasn't even mentioned you to me."

Auldin stepped close to the side of the bed as Hanlon struggled to get up, and pushed him down again. Now Hanlon could see that the mobster was carrying in each hand a piece of large rope, approximately half an inch in diameter and about two feet long. The far end of each was tied into a knot, in which pieces of wires had been woven to add weight.

"Maybe you didn't have anything to do with the arrests," Auldin admitted, "but I still think you did. Anyway, you used me to get in good with Yandor, then turned him against me. I don't like that."

Oh, so that was what had really touched him off. Hanlon saw that the slim man was spoiling for a fight—and that he was using almost any excuse to try to take it out of a fellow who was making good where he had failed.

Hanlon thought, "I don't want to hurt the guy, now that he's down, but I sure don't want to get hurt, either." He had never seen exactly such weapons as Auldin was carrying, but he had a good idea the native was adept in their handling. They looked old and well used.

Hanlon rolled suddenly across the bed and jumped to his feet on the other side. But Auldin ran swiftly around the foot of the bed, and Hanlon was more or less cornered in a narrow space. First one of those strange weapons flicked out, then the other, and Hanlon quickly found out how effective they were. The way Auldin snapped and whipped them made them almost impossible to dodge, and Hanlon felt their burnings across his shoulders—although he was able to protect his face from those first quick flicks.

Hanlon had to get out of that corner, so the next time both ropes flashed out toward him he ducked beneath, down and forward, under Auldin's arms—and was in the center of the room.

The SS man reached out and took over the minds of two of his roches, and made them run between Auldin's legs. Then, as the ropes with those terrible knots at the ends flashed out, Hanlon grabbed them and yanked. The combination of that pull and the roches entangled between his legs was enough to upset the gangster, and he stumbled forward. Hanlon quickly swarmed onto him and got a judo hold on Auldin the man could not break. Holding him thus, Hanlon took the two ropes from his powerless hands, and threw them into a far corner.

"Now get this, and get it straight," Hanlon panted, but as impressively as he could. "I still don't know what this is all about, but I don't like your barging into my room and attacking me like this. Now get out and stay away from me. You try anything like this again, and so help me I'll kill you. And just so you'll remember..." Hanlon put all his pent-up wrath into his fist and threw it at the now-deflated Auldin's jaw. This, he knew, was the only way really to impress a man of that type.

He then forced the half-groggy gangster out of the room and loosed him in the hallway, then shut and locked his door. He listened intently, and finally heard the fellow's mumblings and footsteps going down the stairs. From the window Hanlon watched the thoroughly-frightened native scuttle off down the street, looking furtively all about to see that he was not being followed or observed. Hanlon felt satisfied that he would have no further trouble from him.

As he went back to bed, Hanlon tried to figure this one out. Evidently Auldin did not really know Hanlon had caused those arrests, but was merely using that as an excuse to provoke a fight with one whom he hated for making a success at the same time he, Auldin, was a failure in hiding.

Had Auldin reported this to Yandor? Hanlon had not seen the two together—either through his own or Ebony's eyes—nor had he found anything of the sort in Yandor's mind. But he would have to try to find out that answer, also, among the many others.

He sent his mind back into that of the cat, and took up his spying of the theatrical agent.

About an hour later Yandor had a caller, and Hanlon "listened in" with interest and growing delight. For it was Ovil Esbor, the politician. From the talk between the two, in Yandor's inner, closed office—into which Ebony had also gone—Hanlon got further confirmation of his suspicions. He was more sure than ever now that Yandor was the "top boss" here in Stearra, at least, while Esbor was boss of many other local gangs, including thieves, dope peddlers and panderers.

Hanlon, in his room, made copious notes. "There," he exclaimed after the two men had parted. "That ought to give Morrie enough info to hang 'em. I'll take these notes to him right away."

But Manning was not in his room when Hanlon got there, and since his door was padlocked, Hanlon could not get in. He took a chance and slid his notes under the door.

All this time, however, Hanlon had been watching Yandor through Ebony's mind. He had just barely got back to his apartment when the impresario had another visitor—a masked man. (Hanlon doubted the man had gone through the streets masked—probably had put it on just before entering Yandor's office.)

"Ha! This should be good," and the young SS man paid even closer attention, even as he was putting his motor-trike away, and running up to his room. He heard the two distant men discussing many matters of policy, closeted in that inner room of Yandor's. Hanlon found that the criminal activities were, as he and the other secret servicemen had deduced, planet-wide and under one general control. He knew positively, when this conversation ended, that Yandor was in charge of the activities of this half of the world—the largest continent—and that the masked man was above him in authority.

Was this other kingpin of the whole thing? Or was he, perhaps, what might be termed the "executive director" of the planetary criminal ring? Whatever he was, he was the man Hanlon must get next to and unmask. The Corpsman thrilled. He was gradually but surely climbing that ladder, tediously and maddeningly slow though it seemed sometimes.

"One thing looks sure," Hanlon thought to himself. "Whether or not this bunch is the one that is opposing Estrella's joining the Federation, if we can eliminate them it will mean curbing, if not entirely stopping, this planet-wide crime wave. That'll be worthwhile, even if it's not really our job."

He tried to figure some way to get rid of these two men. If he could lop off the head, the body would die—unless it was a Hydra, with self-regenerating heads.

But after an hour or so of further study and thought, it was borne in upon his consciousness that this was not his job at all. He must quit trying to be the big cheese. If he got any leads, the information must be turned over to his father and the secret service general staff, and let them—not him—worry about how to get rid of these men, or punish them in whatever way Estrellan law provided.

When Hanlon went to the theatre that night, he found Yandor there, with Ebony on its leash—as he had known he would from watching the man through the cat's senses. There was another man with the agent, whom Hanlon had been studying, puzzled by the curious...blocking...in the man's mind. Yandor now introduced him as "my good friend, Egon," and the three chatted together until it was time for Hanlon to go and prepare. Egon complimented him highly on his act, which he said he had seen twice already, and upon the perfect training of his animals.

"How in the name of Zappa do you do it?" he asked. "It's hard enough even to tame roches, to say nothing of training them as you have done."

Hanlon grinned. "Professional secret, nyer." Then he sobered and added, "Actually, it's mainly a matter of hours and days and months of hard work with them, until they know me and like me well enough to do what I tell them, and I know what they are able to do."

He broke away, then, before they could question him further. In his dressing room, while he was putting the uniforms on his dogs and himself, and donning his roch-mask, he pondered seriously a thing that had struck him a stunning blow. For Ebony's mind and delicate senses seemed to detect a distinct similarity between the tones of Egon's voice and those of the masked man—as well as a sameness of effluvia—even though the two spoke in different keys and timbre of voice.

Profoundly stirred, Hanlon studied this seeming fact with intense concentration. How could he make certain?

But his call came just then, and he had to let this new matter rest while he devoted his entire mind to the work of controlling his roches for their act.

Later, in his room, as he again watched Yandor through the cat's eyes, he saw him in his home with Egon and two other men, playing cards, but merely as a group of friends. Nothing whatever was said, during the hours, about any special activities of a criminal nature. No sedition nor revolution was talked; neither Terra nor the matter of Estrella's joining the Federation was so much as mentioned.

Still Hanlon was not sure—and he must become so. Perhaps, he reasoned, the other two men were not in on any of these activities, and for that reason Yandor and Egon could not discuss these matters in their presence. Or perhaps Egon, himself, was not part of Yandor's criminal group after all.

There must be some way of getting proof, Hanlon thought anxiously. How could he positively connect the two, and make sure whether or not the cat's feelings were correct—that Egon was the masked man?

The opportunity came just before the party broke up for the night, many hours later. Egon had picked up the cat and was petting it, as the men were preparing to leave Yandor's house. Not being used to cats, and not knowing the manner in which they like to be petted—rubbing the fur the way it naturally lies down—Egon was ruffling it and rubbing his hands forth and back across Ebony's body.

The cat did not like it. It was only Hanlon's firm control that kept it from... "Hey, that's it!"

He released control of the cat's actions, while still watching through its eyes and ears. Egon's hand again rubbed heavily upward across the cat's fur. Almost light swift was the slash of a clawed paw...and Egon yelped as he dropped Ebony to clap his hand to his chin, on which blood began seeping from several deep and painful scratches.

Egon aimed a hard kick in its direction, but Ebony dodged safely away and ran under a large piece of furniture.

"What happened?" Yandor sprang forward, a cloth in his hand to wipe away the blood from Egon's chin. "Wait a minute. I'll get medicine to put on that."

"Get rid of that cursed animal or I'll kill it," Egon blazed.

"Well now, you must have hurt it some way," Yandor said placatingly as he daubed medicine on his friend's chin, stopping the bleeding and relieving the pain. "Ebony is so friendly and quiet, I can't understand it. He never acted that way before."

"Well, keep the vicious thing caged after this, then," and Egon stomped out of the house, the other two men silently following.

Nor could Hanlon detect anything in Yandor's mind, which he invaded as quickly as possible, that this was anything more than the grumbling of a friend who had been accidentally injured. Yet there was a bit of fear of that other man there, and a resolution to keep the cat out of sight when Egon was around.

Did Yandor, himself, know that Egon and the masked man were the same—or were Hanlon and Ebony wrong? If not, why was Yandor afraid? There were many questions, but no answers—and Hanlon fumed.

He must get facts. He was getting a lot of suspicions and possible clues, and certainly more information all the time. But none of them tied in together as yet; none of them were provable facts.

Slowly, as he thought this out, it became more and more apparent to Hanlon that he must no longer be tied down to his work at the theatre. It—and taking care of the roches daytimes—was demanding entirely too much of his time. Besides, it had only been undertaken to give him a chance to get acquainted with Ino Yandor and, later, to give Hanlon a reason for presenting the cat to this pet collector.

So, when he went to the theatre that night, Hanlon was, to all intents and purposes, roaring drunk. He was surly and insolent to everyone he met, and his performance was terrible. The roches did not stay in straight lines, they were out of step often, and fumbled and stumbled in one way or another much of the time. The master of ceremonies finally came out, forced Hanlon off the stage, then apologized to the stunned audience.

"What made you think you could get away with anything like this?" the manager demanded hotly, down in Hanlon's dressing room. "You're through here—the act is cancelled. And I'll make sure no other theatre hires you."

"Well now, that's right," another angry voice broke in, and Hanlon turned to see Yandor, his face black. "Your entire contract is broken as of now. I'll not tolerate such a disgraceful performance from anyone under me."

Hanlon blustered and cursed, and yanked off his costume to get into his street clothes. He apparently was not concerned with the roches—did not even take off their costumes—but actually he was seeing to it that none of this anger touched their minds or affected them in any way.

Back in his room he considered the matter for some time, and decided he had put it across all right—that these touchy men would not connect him with any reverses they might suffer later in their outside criminal work.

He considered the problem of his roches. He had always loved dogs, and having become so intimate with these Estrellan pooches, he hated to part with them. They were such lovable pets, so gentle and affectionate and loyal. Knowing their minds so intimately, Hanlon knew they had often wondered at the way they were being handled and made to do things beyond their ordinary ability—yet not one of them had ever had the least rebellious thought of ill-feeling toward this master who made them do such unusual things.

But Hanlon knew he could no longer take care of them as they deserved, that they would only be in his way from now on. His first act the next morning after they had been fed, was to see to it that they were taken out and good homes found for them. There were many children living in his own and neighboring houses, who were glad to receive gifts of such fine pets.

That worry solved, Hanlon went back to his room and spent most of the day there, a great deal of it lying down on his bed or sprawled out in his easy chair, his mind in that of Ebony, the cat, or roaming the city watching the minds of the people he knew and suspected.

During the afternoon the masked man called on Yandor again. Through Ebony's sharp eyes Hanlon carefully scrutinized and studied the lower part of the visitor's face, which luckily the mask did not cover.

"Hah!" he exclaimed gleefully. For those scratches were quite plainly visible to one who knew exactly where they were, and who was specifically looking for them, even though it was apparent there had been a careful attempt to conceal them with cosmetics.

Egon and the masked man, then, were one and the same!

But who was he, really? That was Hanlon's next important problem.

The following night, through the cat's eyes, Hanlon again saw Egon and the other two men coming into Yandor's house for one of their usual card games. Now, perhaps, was his chance to find out who the man was, and where he lived.

Ebony had been banished to the next room, but through its ears Hanlon was listening carefully, to know that the four were still in the house. Meanwhile, he dressed and rode his motor-tricycle to the vicinity of Yandor's home. There he hid himself in a dense shadow, always in possession of Ebony's mind, waiting for signs that the men were getting ready to leave.

Unexpectedly, however, as they were going out, a large, ornate, motorized-tricycle with double seats drove up to the house. Egon entered it and was driven rapidly away, far faster than Hanlon's smaller machine could possibly go.

The young SS man was caught flat-footed. Or wait, was he? There was a way, after all...for him.

Swiftly his mind sought about and quickly found a sleeping bird in a nearby tree. Taking control of its mind, he sent it winging after the speeding car, and by this method was able to follow it as it drove swiftly out into the country.

In the spaceship above, a decision was made. By means of the multiphased scanner, certain entities on the planet below, whose general position was already known, were hunted out. For the alien now definitely concluded that they were highly inimical to its plans.

By certain means those beings were captured and taken forcibly to a place that had been prepared.

CHAPTER TEN

IMMEDIATELY AFTER SSM GEORGE HANLON had sent part of his mind into that of a bird and had made it follow Egon's car, the young man followed on his own trike, driven at its top speed out along the road the faster machine had taken.

He cussed the slowness of this clumsy vehicle, wishing he had a fast Terran jet-cycle or car. But he had to make do with what he had, and finally calmed himself with the knowledge that he could see where the other went, through the bird's eyes, even if he himself could not close up the distance separating them.

"You oughta be ashamed of yourself," he scolded himself. "Who else could turn this into success? Be thankful for your great luck in having such a wonderful talent—and quit this eternal griping the minute something goes the tiniest bit haywire."

Thus he saw when the other car turned in through the gates leading to the drive before a rather small, but excellent cottage. The tricycle stopped at the doorway, and Egon got out and entered the house. The chauffeur drove into a shed behind the house, left the machine and then, himself, went into the main house through a back door.

Making the bird peer in through the windows, Hanlon was able to see that this house, while small, was richly and comfortably furnished according to Estrellan standards. By the time he arrived in the vicinity in person, ready to take over the inspection himself, Hanlon had a fairly good idea of the ground floor layout. The upper story was still in darkness, none of the rooms yet lighted.

Hanlon's first act was to direct the bird to a comfortable perch in a nearby tree, close to a semi rotted spot where there were dozens of grubs for its breakfast, and let it go back to sleep. He was always so thankful to his various animal and bird assistants that he was careful to be thoughtful of their ease and well being.

Now, after parking his machine in the shadows of a large flowertree, Hanlon dodged from shadow to shadow, scouting the house and neighborhood carefully.

As best he could judge the estate must be about three acres in extent. There were quite an unusual number of flower beds, and a few quite large flowertrees that should give him considerable cover if he wanted to get closer—which he did not care to risk at this time.

"Mmmm, must be about seven rooms," he mused as he examined the little house. As was usual with Estrellan buildings, it was pentagonal in shape, and with a green-tile roof. Behind it, in addition to the shed where the tricycle was kept, there was another small stone building. But it was dark, and Hanlon could not tell what it was used for.

After seeing all he could from a distance of the outside of Egon's place, Hanlon looked about the neighborhood. It was not too closely built up, but some distance down the street he saw what appeared to be a shopping district. One building was lighted up even at this hour, and he shrewdly guessed it might be a place where men drank. So it proved, and Hanlon entered. While sipping a glass of mykkyl, he did some discreet investigating, both by talking to the serving girl, and by searching the minds of the customers in the cafe.

He was almost rocked back on his heels when he found that the house he had scouted was the home of Adwal Irad—the Second-in-Line.

"Ow!" he yelped mentally. "So Egon and Irad are the same? Where does that put me?"

He again investigated the minds of the few men and women there in the drinking place, looking for thoughts about Irad. Then he left, and slowly rode home, thinking seriously. This was really startling news—and yet, it was half-expected at that. So many clues had pointed that way. So this really meant that Irad was in back of all the pernicious activities that were going on.

But in the name of Snyder, *why!*

That question had him stopped...for the present. Oh, he could think of a dozen reasons, yes. But there was no way—at the moment—of knowing which if any of them was correct. Also, it didn't square with Irad's position, nor with what he had so far learned about the man—not even what his neighbors thought of him, as Hanlon had learned there in the cafe. It was distinctly not in character, and was certainly not what one would expect of the heir to the planetary Rulership.

The next day Hanlon devoted to wandering about the city, hunting for information and thoughts about Adwal Irad. Many times he got into conversation with people of high and low degree, asking questions that forced them to think about the Second-in-Line, so he could read the real thoughts about the man in the minds of these selected people.

Twice he rode his trike to the house where Manning lived, to tell what he had learned and to discuss it with him, but neither time was his fellow operative at home.

Now, the more Hanlon investigated—the more people he talked to and the more minds he studied—the more puzzled he became. Irad just wasn't that kind of a man—at least, he had never been associated in the minds of his future subjects with that sort of thing. He was really well liked. In fact, the general attitude was almost that of hero-worship. And Hanlon knew that where there is hero-worship there first has to be someone worthy of being thought a hero.

Something was screwy somewhere. With what Hanlon was beginning to learn about Irad...

Brash and self-confident as he was, Hanlon knew this was something that must be brought to the attention of his father and the other SS men here. How could he most quickly contact the admiral?

"Manning probably knows exactly how to get in touch with dad," he thought. "He talked with him only a few days ago."

But again Manning was not at home, and Hanlon could not banish the thoughts of worry and frustration from his mind as he rode slowly back to his own rooms. He again set the wakeup on his time-teller for an early hour, and went to sleep. When the call came he hurriedly rose, dressed and breakfasted. Then he went out of his room and the house.

Just as he reached the street and turned toward the part of the city where Manning lived, he swiveled about sharply as he heard the *splat, splat* of running feet coming up behind him. Running—staggering, rather—down the narrow, rutty road was a native, his great feet raising clouds of dust.

Something in the fellow's wild manner held Hanlon's attention. As the runner drew nearer his wildly waving arms and his bloodshot, almost unseeing eyes, told all too plainly that he was badly frightened. Yet, so far as Hanlon could see, nothing or no one was pursuing him.

As the native drew closer, Hanlon gave a start. Why, he knew...but it couldn't be—he was on the Eastern Continent, thousands of miles away. Hanlon's mind must be playing tricks on him. But he scanned the fellow more closely, touching his mind, and at last was sure. It was! Disguised as a native humanoid though he was, Hanlon knew this was Curt Hooper, another of the secret servicemen who was working on this planet.

Hanlon stepped into the road to intercept the runner. He spoke as the man came abreast him, but Hooper paid no attention—seemed not even to see him.

More puzzled than ever, the young SS man ran alongside and reached out to grasp the runner's arm, forcing him to a halt. "Hey, Curt, it's me, Hanlon," he said. "What's the matter?" He was now deeply concerned.

"Don't stop me; gotta run; gotta get away," came gasping Terran words, even as the other tried to loosen himself from Hanlon's grasp.

Hanlon probed quickly into the man's mind but, as usual, he could read only the surface thoughts. These told of some terrible danger threatening—that only running, always running away, could possibly save him.

What the danger was and who or what was threatening him was not in those surface thoughts.

"Snyder help me," Hanlon begged bitterly beneath his breath. Why couldn't he learn how to penetrate deeper into human minds, as he could with animals, and read everything that was there, instead of merely whatever thoughts were passing across the surface?

But Hooper was fighting as only a madman can fight, and Hanlon was barely able to hold him. Yet he must. He *had* to learn what this was all about—why Hooper was here in the Town of the Ruler, instead of back where he had been stationed. What the danger was, and if it threatened the work of the secret servicemen, and possibly the other Terrans. It was clear that Hooper was either drugged or that his mind had become *un*sane in some manner—whether permanently or temporarily, Hanlon could not as yet figure out.

Acting on sudden impulse, Hanlon switched his grasp to a neo-judo hold he had been taught, that made Hooper powerless in his hands. He dragged his companion back inside.

Once in his room Hanlon forced Hooper's unwilling body down on the bed, and pressed certain nerve ends that temporarily paralyzed his body. In this way Hanlon could be more free to study that sick mind, which was not paralyzed, without having to watch every minute lest the deranged man escape him.

While Hanlon was able only to read the surface thoughts, he had learned from experience that by asking leading questions he could often make the other think of things he wanted to know, and this method he now put into practice.

What he learned now, in spite of all the leading questions he could think of to ask, was pitifully meager. Hooper had been made a prisoner and brought to this continent and confined, but had escaped. But he did not know—or could not be made to reveal—why he was on this Western Continent at all, nor how he had been captured or by whom. Hanlon guessed that the man had been held in a small house somewhere fairly near, since he had been running away from there a fairly short time, even though it had seemed an eternity to the frightened man.

Suddenly a stray wisp of thought brought Hanlon upright in his chair.

"Give me that again, Curt!" he demanded, and under his questioning brought out the fact that his father, Admiral Newton, was also a prisoner of these unknowns, as was the fourth member of the SS who had been assigned to Estrella— Morris Manning.

"Mannie couldn't stand the pain, he died," Hooper's thought was strangely calm and apparently heartless—which Hanlon knew could not be the man's true feelings, for Hooper and Manning had been close friends of long standing.

"What kind of pain? Who was hurting him?" Hanlon demanded, sick with dread. "Were all of you being tortured? Was dad?" Oh gawd, *why* couldn't he get in there and read the true answers?

As best he could figure it out, they had never seen their captor, but had felt his mind probing theirs, asking questions, *interrogating* them—in the Estrellan language. Whoever was doing it apparently did not intend it to be torture, for when Manning died the other two received a curiously surprised yet apologetic thought, "Your nerve sensitivity is greater than ours. It was not intended to force this entity's life force out of physical embodiment. Greater care shall be used in the future."

"Tell me more about dad," Hanlon commanded, agonizedly. "Where is he held? Who has him? What's it all about?"

But the dazed Hooper relapsed back to the only words he seemed able to say aloud, "Gotta run; gotta get away."

"But you're safe here, Curt. No one's following you, and I won't let anyone or anything hurt you. Relax."

"Gotta run; gotta get away." And so powerful was the urge that the supine body twitched restlessly, as it began breaking out of that paralysis Hanlon had imposed on it.

Frantically, Hanlon continued his mind scanning, asking innumerable questions that he hoped would penetrate the other's consciousness and force his mind to think along the lines Hanlon wanted to know.

And slowly, sketchily, he began to piece together a picture of sorts—like a jigsaw puzzle of which many of the pieces were missing.

The three SS men had been brought together in some little stone building. There the unknown, whom they never saw nor heard, had interrogated them mentally, a process that was extremely painful in a way that Hooper could not, or did not, specify, save that his mind seemed to wince and recoil from any thought of the method, despite Hanlon's utmost attempts to learn it.

There seemed to have been days and nights of this painful questioning, although Hooper could not tell exactly how long— and Hanlon knew it could not have been very many days, since he had seen Manning so recently.

Then, early this morning, shortly after Manning's death, and while Hooper was being questioned, it seemed to him the mental voice had gone away abruptly, leaving him in full command of his senses. He had immediately begun to examine the room, and soon found that the low door was unfastened. Cautiously he opened it and discovered that it opened to the outside of the building. The admiral had not been in the room with him at the time, nor could Hooper find a way into the other parts of the building—if there were any other parts to it.

Therefore, he had lost no time in leaving by that providentially open door. He started running across a lawn toward the nearest road. Down this he ran, knowing only a terrified compulsion to run, to hide, to get away from that horrible inquisition.

"How long have you been running?" Hanlon asked sympathetically, yet in hopes it might give him a clue.

"Gotta run; gotta get away," Hooper's words said, but the thought flashed across his mind, "since after dawn."

"Then dad's not too far away," Hanlon thought, and began trying to guess where or in what direction the prison might be, and how he could locate it most quickly.

He was awakened to reality to see Hooper rise from the bed, the paralysis broken by that inner compulsion to flee. Before Hanlon could jump up to stop him, Hooper was out of the room.

Hanlon let him go. He hated to do it, but there was no apparent way he could save Hooper now...and he *had* to get to his father just as fast as he could. Not only because the admiral was his adored dad, but because he was second in command of the whole I-S C's secret service, and in charge of this mission, and thus the more important at the moment.

"But where is he?" Hanlon's thoughts were an agonized wail. For the first time in months he felt very young, and inexperienced, and unsure.

He jumped to his feet to leave the house and start searching, but restrained himself before he got to the door. "Whoa, boy, not so fast. I haven't got the faintest idea where dad is. Must think this out first, and not waste a lot of time during which he might die or be killed."

He sank back into his chair again, and his mind swiftly reviewed the pitifully small bits of information he had been able to glean from the deranged mind of his friend Hooper.

Someone, or something, or some group, who were the main support of this opposition, had a mental ability Hanlon thought he knew the Estrellans did not have. At least, he had not found any traces of it anywhere here. Or, wait now. Did the Rulers have it? Was this one of the traits and abilities especially bred into them in the course of making them capable of handling their tremendous task of being Planetary Ruler? Could be. He had not yet had the chance to scan mentally Elus Amir, the present Ruler, except for that one night at the theatre, and then he had not really tried to see what the man had in the way of mental equipment. Hanlon had been so relieved to find he and the audience were applauding instead of booing that he had not tried to do so.

If Elus Amir as Ruler had it, did Adwal Irad as Second-in-Line also have those mental powers?

Whoever or whatever it was—and that would have to be studied more thoroughly later—some mind or minds had forced the other three secret servicemen to go to a certain place...at present unknown to Hanlon...and had there imprisoned them and tried to extract information from their minds.

Information about what...and why? What could these unknowns want to know that couldn't be learned by asking direct questions? For the Federation statesmen and Survey men had been glad and anxious to answer fully and truthfully every question that had been asked of them.

And that puzzling thought Hooper had said they received when Manning died. "Your nerve sensitivity is greater than ours—we had not realized it would kill you to be thus interrogated." Or words to that effect. As far Hanlon knew the native Estrellans did not have unusual resistance to pain. He had had several encounters with them so far, and had known cases where they were hurt or wounded and had not noticed any great immunity to pain. Was this, then, another special attribute of the Rulers? But Egon, or Irad, had certainly felt pain when Ebony scratched his chin, and had made quite a fuss about it. Was it real—or was he "putting on an act" to conceal his immunity. Somehow, Hanlon was not willing to accept that last.

Dimly, in the back of his mind, there seemed to be another puzzling thought. What was it? Hanlon worried at it like one of the roches might worry a bone...and finally it struck him—hard.

If the other three had been captured, why hadn't he?

At its multiphased scanner in the spaceship high above, the being stiffened suddenly. For long minutes, the mind concentrated on this new problem. The plan put into operation that morning had been partially successful. The "location" of that unreadable mind before noticed, found once and then lost—was now known again.

But still, despite every effort, contact with that mind could not be made.

After a time, therefore, with the utmost precision a thought was insinuated into the Estrellan mind constantly being held captive. The thought was seen to take hold, then its strength and urgency was increased.

Soon although the native was at a loss to account for the reason why such a thought should come to him at that particular time, he nevertheless sent a note to a certain person, giving forceful orders that were to be obeyed immediately.

CHAPTER ELEVEN

AT THAT THOUGHT, FEAR STRUCK AT GEORGE Hanlon's vitals, almost like a physical blow. What was planned for *him*?

For certainly if these unknowns were onto what the Terrans—or the Corps and the secret service—were trying to do here, and had already captured and tortured three of the four, they would not leave him free to continue working against them.

Cold sweat starting from all his pores, Hanlon sank into a chair, nails digging into palms. His bravado, his cockiness, his belief in his own superiority—all ebbed away like a swift-falling tide.

He had been used to working alone in the service. He had been mostly by himself on Simonides, and altogether alone on

Algon. Yet he had not felt such an *aloneness,* such an absolute withdrawal of all support, as he knew in this awful moment.

For at the other places he could contact the SS through the safety deposit boxes, or by the "Andromeda Seven" password, and get almost instant response, and the entire resources of the Corps to back him up. And here on Estrella, while he had been working alone, he met the others occasionally, and the men with the Corps' sneakboat every fortnight. He had known they were *there.*

But now they were gone. And Hanlon was to be the next victim…and he had no idea who, when, what, where, or why.

For long minutes he sat, shaking with dread, his mind a chaos of nothingness but a swirling, roiling, panic-fear.

This was far, far different from that terrible fear he had known back on the *Hellene* when he had first realized he was tangling with trained, unprincipled and viciously conscienceless killers. Or the time he had been chained in the Prime Minister's dungeon on Simonides. For then he had been facing known problems. This one was totally unknown…and man has always felt far more fear of the terrors he cannot see, than of those he can face.

"Blast back," he thought determinedly, ashamed of his fear and resolved to conquer it. "I got through those other troubles all right in the end. How do I know I won't with this? At least I can be a man, not a cry baby, especially before I'm actually in danger."

It was sorry advice, and he knew it, but it was just enough at the moment to help him pull himself together.

"So maybe they can kill me…after torturing me. So what? I don't expect to live forever, and I knew when I got into this service that it was dangerous. After all, I could get killed any minute just performing routine Corps duties—or if I'd remained a civilian, at my daily job, or walking the streets of Terra."

By main force of will and character, Hanlon forced the fear back and away from the surface of his mind. He concentrated on the problem at hand—how to find where his father was held captive.

Hooper had apparently been running for about two hours when Hanlon first discovered him, his mind had told. All right, where's that map of Stearra and vicinity he had bought. Ah, there on the table. Let's see now, a man in Hooper's condition could run maybe ten or twelve miles in that time, since his mental terror would have overcome physical fatigue until his muscles could absolutely obey no longer.

All right, circle this point with a ring with a twelve-mile radius…so.

But Curt was coming from the south. Concentrate on that direction for the moment. What lies ten to twelve miles from here to the south?

He examined the map carefully, trying to visualize in his mind what layout in that direction. The Ruler's palace was more or less south, but nearer to fifteen miles. Could Hooper have run that far since dawn? Hanlon didn't think so, though the man had so evidently been running until almost exhausted.

The section Hanlon was visualizing was, he remembered now, mostly filled with the larger homes and estates of the more influential and wealthy.

Yandor's house? No, that was more to the west, and only about two miles from here. Of course Hooper could have been circling and zigzagging during those hours—oh, but not that much, surely.

Carefully Hanlon pored over the map, trying to figure where his father could possibly be held.

Suddenly, a bit to the east, and about eleven miles from the street where Hanlon lived, he noticed a penciled dot he had previously made on the map.

Irad's house!

Of course, Hanlon gasped. And that enigmatic stone building—Hooper had thought "stone"—behind the house. Also, all indications up to the present pointed toward the

Second-in-Line as the head man of the criminal element…and that probably meant of the opposition, as well.

But Hooper's thoughts had been that the SS men's torture and inquisition had been mental. Did Irad have that power? Hanlon had asked himself that before, but now it became increasingly evident that he did, he must have. Besides, now that Hanlon was concentrating on the subject, there had been that curious sensation of a mental block or barrier Hanlon thought he had felt in Egon-Irad's mind. What was behind that curtain?

"Well," Hanlon shivered, "there's only one way to find out. I'll have to scout this place more closely, and see if he's *it.*"

He rose determinedly to start out. But halted as he realized it was broad daylight, and that he could not go there and investigate the house and grounds—and that stone building in the back—without being seen. He would have to take this slow and easy. Too much depended on him and there was very little chance of his making it undiscovered even under the best of circumstances. He must not take chances that he knew beforehand were doomed to failure. For he was now the sole and only possibility of his father being freed. That sneakboat was not due for another week and a half and with Manning and Hooper out of the picture…

Chafing at the delay, his mind a turmoil of tortured thoughts, conflict between his desire to rush and the logical knowledge that he must wait until dark, Hanlon passed the most miserable time of his young life. He had thought he had plumbed the depths of mental agony during those dreadful seven minutes when he had stood at rigid attention in the office of Admiral Rogers, commandant of cadets. But that had been a mere child's game compared to all this fretful waiting.

But those deep, inner and innate characteristics that made George Hanlon what he was, came to the fore during those hours, as he forced himself to endure the wait he knew he must accomplish.

And in that period George Hanlon reached closer to full maturity. He touched, examined and accepted the tremendous concept that man's highest pinnacle of success, his greatest heights of achievement in personal integration, lay in working with others for the common good of all, not in feeling that anyone man is indispensable; one man—himself, of course—better than others, and more capable than they of achieving all goals.

Sure, he had an ability none of the others had. But that did not make him any better than, nor above them. They, in turn, had many capabilities he did not possess, that were actually as valuable as his mental abilities—if not more so. As an individual, any of them could fail. As a *team*, each giving of his best, they could win out.

And now someone or some group had broken up the team. Well, it was up to him to get it back together again.

George Hanlon suddenly awoke. He sprang from his chair, astonished to see through the window of his room that it was dark outside. He grinned mirthlessly. He had actually fallen asleep there in his chair, in the midst of all his worry.

Then suddenly he realized why. He had thought the matter through, reached definite conclusions, and had known, inwardly, that everything was now as it must be until a certain time. Thus calmed and facing that fact, however unconsciously, he had fallen asleep to gain strength for that coming ordeal. Now it was time to go, therefore he had awakened.

He took another half-hour to prepare and eat a good meal—he would need all the strength he could get—then left his room and the house. Mounting his trike, he sped away at its swiftest pace toward the neighborhood where Adwal Irad's house lay.

The alien, watching from above in its scanners, saw that entity with the unreadable mind leave its home and start away on its mechanical carrier. Tracing its course, the being was soon able to make a shrewd guess as to its destination.

Instantly the alien's mind went into action, and under its compulsion four armed men hastened to Irad's house, and hid themselves within its partially-darkened interior, yet kept careful watch of the outside premises.

Hanlon had long since decided just how to approach the place. Leaving his machine concealed in the deep shadows of a spreading flowertree, he slipped quietly through the edge of the grounds next door, dodging from tree to tree to bush, carefully watching all about to make sure he was not seen nor followed.

He came to a large tree close to the Irad property, hurdled a low hedge and dashed across the dividing line, to come to a stop beneath another tree well into the grounds of the Second-in-Line. From that one he made his cautious, soundless way, until he was only about ten yards from the house itself.

There were only a couple of lights showing through the windows, but his heart sank at the realization that someone was at home.

"I should have had a bird watching to see if Irad left," he scolded himself. But he continued on, making a final dash across the remaining yardage until he was right beside the house itself, in a deep shadow.

Carefully he inched his way along toward the nearest window from which a light showed. Reaching it he very slowly rose and peered through the lower corner of the pane.

This was apparently a sort of living room or library, as he could see a number of easy chairs, carbide lamps on standards for reading, a couple of small tables with art objects or flowers on them. Along one wall were recesses holding reading scrolls. But there was no one in the room he could see.

He crept on to another window, and repeated his inspection. This one was a bedroom, but again no one was there.

"Maybe Irad just leaves a couple of lights on when he's away," Hanlon considered. He crept on to another window, but there was no light and he could not see what was within. He rounded a corner of the five-sided house, going toward the back, but there were no lighted windows in that side. He ran along it to the back, noting as he did so that he passed a closed door.

He now was close to that little stone building at the rear, which he had previously noted, and in which he was sure his father was imprisoned. There was no light showing and apparently no windows at all. He ran toward it swiftly, and ducked into its shadow. He circled it completely, but there was only one door-locked.

George Hanlon probed with his mind toward the interior, and faintly, just barely on the threshold of his consciousness, he caught a familiar thought-pattern.

"It is dad," he exulted, but silently. Almost forgetting caution, he doubled back and was attacking that locked door, when a sound behind made him whirl about.

A number of men were boiling swiftly out of that door in the main house he had passed a few moments before. And the light now shining out reflected on the unmistakable flameguns in their hands. In that first quick glance he had recognized Yandor as one of the men.

"Yipe!" Hanlon knew a deep disappointment—which did not stop him from starting away from there on a dead run. He increased his speed as he heard the pounding of heavy feet behind him.

He dashed toward the nearest yard, trying always to keep in the shadows. Fortunately, he was fleeter than his pursuers, and gained considerable yardage on them.

Around that next house he ran, and across the next yard. A couple of flamegun flashes sprang out at him, but not close. The gangsters were also flashing the lights from reflector lanterns, trying to locate and spotlight him for more accurate shooting.

In the drive of that neighboring house Hanlon saw one of the Estrellan motor-trikes. It took him but a moment to activate the engine that, for a wonder, caught almost immediately. He jumped onto the seat and was picking up speed as he reached the street and swung down it.

Behind he heard an outcry as the owners saw the theft of their machine. Also, the angry yells of the men chasing him.

These little tricycles were made for local trips only, and were not powered for speed or distance. The best he was able to coax out of the acetylene-powered engine was about twenty miles an hour.

He had not gone a mile before he heard behind him the sound of one of the larger trikes, whose greater-sized motor, he knew, had a top speed of nearly thirty miles an hour.

Pushing his little machine as fast as it would go, Hanlon looked wildly all about him for some place of safety. He knew he had only a few minutes before the bigger trike would catch up with him—or at least be within shooting distance.

But how had they known he was coming? They must have been lying in wait, to have taken him so completely off guard. Else why or how could they have been hiding in semi-darkness, to come rushing out of that door, their flamers ready to cinder him?

A momentary blackness of fear struck at him, but he threw it off by an effort of will. They hadn't caught him yet; and by the great John Snyder, they wouldn't!

Hah! Off there to the left was a little patch of woods.

And just ahead was a corner. He made as though to keep straight on, then swerved at the last moment toward the left. His tires shrieked at the sudden braking and swift turn. The little machine almost overturned—but he made it.

Glancing back he saw the larger, swifter tricycle hurtle past the corner he had so unexpectedly turned. That would give him a little extra leeway, before they could stop, turn around, and come back down the road he was on.

Soon he reached the beginning of the wood, and was in the shadows its trees cast across the road. Luckily, he thought, his little machine had no lights, and it would be that much harder for them to spot him in the darkness.

He went a little farther, then slowed a bit, swung his right leg over onto the left side of the trike, and threw himself off, allowing it to continue on without him. How far it would go, unguided, he did not know, but hoped it would be some distance.

Glancing backward over his shoulder as he ran, he saw the lights of the gangster's car pass. For some minutes he continued running, zigzagging a bit around the trees, hoping to get far enough away so they could not find him. As he ran he continued thinking what had happened.

"Were those goons actually waiting for me?" It didn't seem possible anyone could have suspected him, personally, or have had any idea he was going to be around Irad's house tonight. How could they, possibly. He hadn't told anyone. That unknown mind power again?

Memory of that *someone* with the extraordinary mental powers, who had captured and imprisoned and questioned the other SS men, came to him and again, involuntarily, he shuddered.

It probably was not that one or ones; he tried to deny the belief. Undoubtedly those gun-carrying men were merely guarding the house on general principles, either because Irad was Second-in-Line, or else because...

"Gosh, I almost forgot. I'm sure dad's there, for those were his thoughts I was just beginning to catch, I know. His mind texture is unmistakable. I'll bet those guys were there as guards for that reason. I'll have to..."

He stopped short and dodged behind a tree, for his quick ear had caught a crackling in the underbrush behind him. He tried to peer out through the dimness, but could not see anyone, although he could see two or three lances of lights that he knew were the reflectors of the gangsters.

"I didn't realize they'd get this close this quick," he almost wailed. "I gotta get out of here, but fast."

He started off as quietly as he could. But there were so many fallen leaves and dead twigs and branches underfoot that he could not help making some noise.

Suddenly a lance of flame almost caught him. He dodged quickly again. There was another shot in his general direction that did not hit him—but it did touch a dried, dead branch.

Instantly there was a flare of light as the wood caught fire, and in moments a considerable blaze was started that made further concealment impossible. Only flight was left.

Hanlon turned and ran toward the farther edge of the wood. Behind him he could hear footsteps rapidly following, and a voice bellowing, "Here he is!"

CHAPTER TWELVE

GEORGE HANLON RAN AS HE HAD NEVER RUN before, but somehow, surprisingly, that Estrellan native not only kept up with him, but the young SS man could tell from the sound that he was catching up. This guy must be half greyhound, Hanlon thought—although he, himself, was slowed down by those huge shoes to which he was not yet too accustomed, so that when running he had trouble not stumbling over his own feet. It was hard remembering to keep his legs spread further apart than normal.

He finally saw just ahead of him the far edge of the woods, and beyond that a great, open meadow. He would be in clear sight out there, unless he could outdistance his pursuers. And this closest one was much too near for that. He would have to stop this gunnie somehow, and now.

Hanlon ducked behind a great tree, and peered out carefully. In his hands he held a knob of wood he had picked up. Soon he saw the native come running between the trees, straight in his direction.

Hanlon took a firmer grip on his club, and raised it above his head. The mobster came alongside the tree; the club came down—hard. One down.

Hanlon started on across the meadow then, for the woods was afire and he felt there was no chance of escape that way. He hoped he could find some sort of a hiding place out there—quite sure in his mind he could not out-distance the men following. He zigzagged a bit as he ran, and kept looking back over his shoulder from time to time.

Hanlon had covered nearly two hundred yards, and was again looking back over his shoulder, when suddenly his foot struck something, and he pitched headlong. The breath *whooshed* out of him as he landed. He felt as though he was a mass of cuts and bruises. He fought to regain his breath, drawing in great gulps of air. His back hurt, and his legs. One arm seemed almost useless.

"Oh no, not broken!" he wailed inwardly. Tentatively he tried to move it, and found to his joy that it was only badly jammed. He remembered now, he had landed on that hand.

He glanced around and saw that he had fallen over a great, exposed rock-edge, perhaps a foot high, half as wide, but eight or nine feet long. Despite the inconvenience of dozens of pieces of broken rock on the ground there, he swung his body around so he was lying along the length of the rock, hoping thus to hide a bit while he regained his breath and a measure of strength.

"If I'm lucky I can hide here until they leave," he panted, striving to calm his nerves and slow his breathing. He peered cautiously over the top of the rock, back toward the burning wood.

Soon he saw another of the men emerge carefully from the edge of the wood, but a considerable distance away. He watched this fellow as he crept out into the meadow, looking from side to side in his search for their quarry.

So intent was Hanlon on watching this man that he did not see nor hear the approach of a third man, until the other jumped the stone, almost landing on Hanlon. The SS man could not entirely stifle an exclamation, and instantly the man swiveled and shone his light directly on Hanlon.

Swiftly the Corpsman snaked out his hand, caught the goon's foot and yanked. The man fell backward, and Hanlon, injuries forgotten, leaped up. But with a lithe, swift movement his attacker was on his feet, swinging at Hanlon with the hand holding his lantern. It was, the SS man saw now, the fellow he thought he had knocked out with his club.

The Terran's hands darted out and grabbed the man's other wrist, pushing it up and away. For in the gyrations of the lamp he had seen that the fellow carried a flamer.

Forth and back they wrestled. By dint of extra effort Hanlon kept the gun's muzzle pointed away from him. But he realized sickeningly that his antagonist was stronger and heavier than he. For an Estrellan, this goon was really a giant.

Hanlon decided on a desperate chance. Instead of pushing *against* the man's strength, he suddenly lunged backward. The goon cursed as he strove to keep his own footing, and pulled back as best he could.

Hanlon's reflexes were faster than the mobster's, and he took full advantage of the change of leverage. He twisted half-sideways, and let go with his right hand. He swung with all his strength at the soft belly before him.

The man grunted and tottered, for he had not quite regained full equilibrium. Again and again Hanlon struck. The man staggered, reeled backward. A quick snatch and Hanlon had the flamer…and used it.

Swiftly he looked to see if the man he had been watching had noticed the fight—and the flash.

Apparently he had, for he was coming on a run. Hanlon snapped a shot at him—and missed. An answering lance of flame almost got him. Hanlon tried another…and got only a weak sizzle. The first gunman's flamegun was dead.

Only flight was left. Hanlon dropped the useless weapon and started off across the field as fast as he could run. He had not fully recovered his breath, and every muscle in his body shrieked from that fall and his unusual exertions.

He stumbled and staggered, but kept on running as fast as he could. Behind he could hear the yells of the gunman who was on his trail, apparently calling to someone else. The beam of the lantern held Hanlon almost steadily.

Still the Corpsman ran. He had no idea what lay ahead, or whether he was running toward safety or into more danger. There was no other cover he could see in the almost dark—no trees nor bushes. Merely this meadow, almost flat, covered with a sort of blossomy grass not more than two or three inches high. Nor even if he did find something, would he be long concealed from the lantern and the man who carried it.

Hanlon swerved, and ran toward but behind the lantern-carrier, hoping thus to elude him. In fact, he had passed behind the fellow before the light rays picked him out again.

The beam held him steadily again, and Hanlon could hear those pounding feet coming nearer. A gun flamed out again, and Hanlon felt the excruciating pain of a burn on the side of his arm.

"Yipe, that was close," he gritted as he clamped his other hand over the wound, and tried to increase his speed. Weariness seemed forgotten for the moment, and he was able to spurt ahead.

Suddenly he saw twin beams of stronger light coming across the field to intercept him. "Oh no," he gasped, "the trike!"

He swerved sharply to the right again, and ran on. Ahead he heard a strange sort of roar, and only after a moment or so could identify it. It sounded like the boom of breakers.

"Am I that near the sea?"

Again a sword of flame almost caught him. The car was roaring toward him, closer each second. He knew starkly that death or capture was a matter of moments only.

His mind had been reaching out, searching for any sort of animal life that might come to his assistance. But in this hour of need even that avenue of help seemed to have detoured.

That roar sounded closer—yet curiously distant. Yet he was almost sure it was the sound of breaking water. "If it's close enough, maybe I can find safety there. It's my only hope now," he prayed.

He pounded on and suddenly, almost straight ahead the nearer of Estrella's two moons swung above the horizon. Both moons were far closer to Estrella than Luna was to Terra. Neither was nearly as large, but they gave considerable light, and this nearer moon was almost at the full tonight. Hanlon could see better now—but he knew his pursuers could, too, and that he was now plain in their sight.

"Sorry, dad, but it looks like I've failed," he groaned.

The sound of the water was closer now, and it had more the texture of breakers than of surf. He devoutly hoped so. Breakers would mean rocks, and rocks would be hard to avoid if he had to dive. But, more important, they would mean greater chances for safety if this meadow ran directly into them, so he could find a hiding place.

Now both gunmen behind were closer. They were firing steadily—and even in his anxiety to escape Hanlon found time to sneer at their marksmanship. "Wish I had a gun or a blaster— I'd show them some real shooting."

Almost blinded now with fatigue, and his run barely more than a stagger, he struggled on…and suddenly skidded to a halt just on the lip of a sharp drop off. He peered downward, and his heart did flip-flops. This cliff was well over a hundred and fifty feet high-and straight down to the water's edge. It was the slapping of the water against it he had heard.

Even in the moon's rays he could see that it was too vertical, too smooth, for a swift downward climb. He looked wildly to right and to left, but could see no possible safety.

The car with its gunmen was closer now, and one of the flames from their guns almost hit him. There was only one possible escape.

He ran back from the cliff's edge for several yards, straight toward the onrushing car. Then he turned and sprinted for that edge. He took off like a broad jumper, as far outward as he could, curving his body downward into a dive.

"Oh, Lord, please," he prayed earnestly, "deep water and no rocks."

It seemed an interminable age that George Hanlon fell through the air on that incredible dive toward the water so far away. Not knowing what was below made the moments seem dreadful eternities. His mind persisted in painting ghastly pictures…

At long last Hanlon struck—and was instantly numbed from the force of the blow and chilled by the icy water. His bruises, burns, and cuts smarted painfully from the salt. He plummeted into the depths, deeper, deeper, until he thought his lungs would burst, despite the great gulp of air he had breathed in just before he hit. Slowly he let out a little bit—and as he sank ever deeper, a bit more. He just couldn't take it any longer. He would have to let go soon, and try to breathe.

But from some hidden source he drew on new reserves of will and of strength, and fought on. He felt his descent slowing, and clawed his way upward.

His head finally burst through the surface, and he trod water while he gratefully gulped in the reviving air.

All at once he heard a sharp *ping,* and water splashed in his face. One of those goons above had a pellet gun.

Hanlon struck out away from the shore, swimming under water as fast and as far as his breath and strength would allow, coming up only to gulp another lung full of air, then submerging again. Finally he surfaced and looked back toward the cliff top. He could dimly see three forms standing there.

Another pellet struck close by…and another. Why, he wondered, hadn't they used that gun on him before?

Never too strong a swimmer, the exhaustion and weakness of his wounds and that long run made swimming almost impossible for the young secret serviceman. But he knew his life—and the success of his mission here—depended on his keeping going. He kicked off the heavy, water logged special shoes that made his feet look Estrellan. Ridding himself of their weight helped a little.

He had felt hundreds of tiny waves of strange thought beating at the fringes of his mind, and now he opened it wide to receive these impressions.

"Fish," he said disgustedly after a moment, as he kept swimming further out. "What good…?" He stopped and thought carefully. "If it was a big enough fish, maybe…" He sent his mind purposefully out and around.

He was still trying to swim, but his body was worn out.

He knew desperation, for even if he outdistanced their pellets, there was just not enough strength left in him to swim back to shore. He turned over on his back and floated, resting as much as possible, but still kept his mind searching, searching through the waters. It was his only chance, he felt sure, and sent it ever farther out.

Finally he contacted a larger, stronger thought. Avidly he seized it, insinuated his mind into it, and realized at once that it was the brain of a fish. He forced it to swim at its top speed toward him. From the size and texture of the mind it felt like a large fish. He hoped it was big enough.

Soon it came up to him, and he saw that it was shark-like, almost eight feet long, but rounder, and with a head and face much like that of a Terran sea-elephant. Eagerly and thankfully he grasped one of the small fins protruding from its underside, and his mind started it swimming along parallel to the coast.

The musket-type gun had been *splatting* at him from time to time—evidently as fast as the shooter could reload. He looked up toward the cliff top, and could see men running along it.

"Must be they can see me," although he doubted if they could see the fish, that swam just below the surface. "Probably," he said, grinning mirthlessly, "they're wondering how I can swim so fast."

Another pellet plowed into the water close ahead of his face. The portion of his mind inside the fish felt the intolerable, burning shock of pain. The fish seemed almost to stumble. It twisted and coiled about until Hanlon was able to tighten his control and calm it.

In the dim moonlight he could see the water becoming discolored—and knew the fish was bleeding profusely.

His mind in the fish knew where the wound was, and Hanlon reached up for that place and found a gaping hole. He put the tip of a finger into it to stop the bleeding as much as possible. But he realized at once that this would not save his carrier, which by now he knew was not a true fish, but an amphibious mammal, just as Terran's whales are mammals, not fish.

What could he do? As weak as he was, and as poor a swimmer as he was at best, there was absolutely no chance of his making it back to shore under his own power. And even if he did get back, there was no beach, only that unscalable rocky escarpment…and the gunmen on top of that.

The fish was his only hope, for he had not been able to locate another fish-mind of the same calibre. And now his savior was dying.

More carefully now, with his mind inside the amphibian, he examined the structure of its brain and nervous and muscular systems. Would it be possible to close that terrible wound?

He traced the nerves to the muscles of that portion of the body and skin. He tested and tried everything he could figure out.

Finally Hanlon found the nerve-muscle combination that controlled exactly that portion of the body. He made it contract—and felt the muscle tighten about his fingertip. Gently he withdrew the latter from the wound, and made the muscles close it tightly and completely. It was necessary to keep doing it consciously, for the moment he relaxed his concentration it opened again.

He noted subconsciously that there had been no more shots for some time. "Maybe the guy's outa bullets," he thought. "Or perhaps they think I'm dead—can see the blood-stains and think they're mine. Or maybe," as an afterthought, "they've lost track of me in the dimness and the choppy waters."

Whatever the reason, Hanlon knew a deep thankfulness. He relaxed as best he could, shivering in the icy waters, still holding loosely onto the fin of the fish-thing.

He did not try to make it swim. In fact, he kept it from doing so. He would take time out to try to regain some of his own strength, while letting the fish overcome, if possible, some of its own weakness and shock from the pellet-wound.

Adwal Irad had been growing strangely worried. Acting on a compulsion he did not realize existed, he moved Admiral Newton to a different and—a certain being in a spaceship high above hoped—a more concealed place of imprisonment.

CHAPTER THIRTEEN

"IF I WAIT HERE AWHILE, PERHAPS THE FISH'S strength will build up again," George Hanlon had thought wearily. "Then it can carry me back to shore."

So he continued concentrating on the job of keeping those muscles closed around the wound in the amphibian's side, finding it required full use of his mind to think of holding that constriction, and of nothing else.

Only partially was that possible, of course. Humans are just not constituted so they can think of only one thing for long periods of time. "At least," he grimaced, "not this human."

For nearly an hour he and the fish lay there quietly, riding out the waves, while he waited for the great mammal-thing to regain some of its energy. He kept close watch of that mind, and knew it was gradually feeling less pain, less anguish. He had sent it "calming" thoughts as best he could, and they had taken effect. The panic was gone. It was almost asleep, floating there.

Hanlon looked toward the cliff top, but there were no longer figures there he could see. Had the pursuers, thinking him dead, left? He strained his ears for the sound of the trike motor.

"Maybe, though, they'd already gone before I thought to start listening," he thought.

Finally he decided the fish was strong enough to take him to shore. His own body felt so much more comfortable. Then he realized with a twinge of panic that the reason was that while he had thrown his mind into the healing of the fish his body had become numb with the cold. Now he again became conscious of his various cuts and bruises, aching and flaming from the action of the salt water.

Under his compulsion the fish swam slowly and with some difficulty back toward the shore. When it finally got close to the wall of rock Hanlon let his feet downward, hoping to be able to touch bottom. But the water was far too deep there.

"I hate to do this to you, fellow, but you're my only hope for the time being," Hanlon said feelingly to the great fish-thing, and made it start swimming along the rocky wall. He kept his eyes constantly looking ahead for a break in the escarpment, or for a bit of beach where he could rest.

After a mile or so it seemed the cliff was getting lower, and Hanlon's hopes rose a bit. Another couple of thousand yards, and he was sure of it. It was sloping downward quite sharply toward sea level. Also it seemed, in the moonlight, that the rocky surface was getting rougher, more climbable.

Finally they came to a place where the cliff was only about twenty yards high—nor did it seem to get lower on ahead. Too, it looked scalable. Hanlon stopped the fish and examined that facing carefully.

Yes, he decided at last, there were enough protuberances and cracks so that it could be climbed.

If he had strength enough.

"Well, gotta try sometime. And my poor fish is about all done." He made it swim right up until he could reach out and get a firm grip in a large crack.

"Goodbye, fellow. Thanks for saving my life. Hope you make out all right," he told the great mammalian shark-thing. He released his hold on its fin and his control from its mind. It turned and swam away, still feebly.

Hanlon focused his attention on the task before him. Slowly and painfully he climbed, hunting for handhold and footrest.

He had known he was tired, but had not realized how weak he was. It seemed he could never make even that short climb. His fingers, hands and arms were numb with cold, his feet and legs unresponsive leaden weights. But from the deeps of his subconscious and will, and his urge to survival, he brought renewed strength and scrambled upward.

At last, utterly spent, he pulled himself over the edge, and lay gasping and shivering on the top of the cliff.

He was almost ready to blank out, when a thought struck him, and he struggled to retain consciousness. He could not just lie here and sleep. Probably those goons would still be looking for him. He must get away, somehow, somewhere.

Again he sent his mind outward, and felt whispers of thought quite a little distance away across the meadow. He followed the strongest of these, and found a mind quite powerful, and intelligent in an animalistic way.

He followed that mind into the brain that housed it, and took control. He made the animal, whatever it was, start swiftly toward him. While it was coming he examined the mind more closely, and suddenly realized he was inside the brain of an Estrellan *caval*.

These animals, which the Terrans thought of as horses, because they could be ridden or trained to draw carriages, were about the size of a Terran cow-pony. They were striped almost like a zebra, but the colors were brown and yellow, rather than black and white. The animals were quite vicious in the wild state, and none too tractable even when trained. As usual with Estrellan animals, they were tail-less, and had heavy, sharp hooves, nearly twice the size of those of Earthly horses, and snouts much like a roch's.

When the caval came up to him, Hanlon saw it was a stallion, slightly larger than average. From its mind he already knew it was a wild one, not domesticated or broken to saddle or harness.

Nevertheless, he could control it, and made it stand quietly while he climbed slowly and laboriously to his feet, and from there managed to wriggle onto its back.

He knew he was due to faint in a few seconds, but kept his consciousness long enough to impress on the animal's mind that it was to take him back toward Stearra. He thought he knew the direction, and he thought he could keep awake the one part of his mind that was dissociated and in the caval. However, because he might blank out completely, he instructed it to keep straight on the road to town.

He leaned down and threw his arms tightly about the caval's neck, then with a sigh of thankfulness, let himself go. He had endured so much…he was so tired…so…tir…

Yandor and his men had finally come to the conclusion that Gor Anlo was dead, out there in the ocean. They had been unable to see him for some time. Yet they waited around for nearly half an hour, searching both the waters and along the cliff. Finally, he said they might as well go home. So all piled in their large trike and started back to the city.

But they had not quite reached his home when Yandor found a disturbing thought persisting in his mind. He worried and puzzled over it for some time, then issued sharp commands. Thus, when they arrived at his house, two of the men hurried into the back yard, and soon came back with two of the beasts Yandor kept caged there.

"What's up, chief?" one of the men asked as the tricycle sped back the way they had just come.

"I…I don't really know," the impresario said slowly. "I…I have a…a sort of feeling…that maybe we can find Anlo after all. We'd better go back and look some more."

For the watcher above knew Hanlon was not dead.

All of George Hanlon's mind must have become unconscious, for the next thing he knew was when the caval suddenly reared to escape those who were trying to stop it, and Hanlon's body was dumped unceremoniously to the ground. The caval, released from its compulsion, took off across the meadow at top speed.

Hanlon began to recover consciousness as rough hands slapped him awake. He first noticed that the sun was rising, for its rays were shining directly in his eyes. He blinked and turned his head away—and became aware of his captors.

He saw Ino Yandor standing there, beside a large trike. Beside him was one of his henchmen, holding the leashes of two straining *tamous*. These cat-like beasts, somewhat like Terran black panthers save they were a deep red in color, and had fangs much longer and sharper—and no tails—Hanlon knew to be trackers *par excellence*—as good as bloodhounds. Nor were they usually as fierce and bloodthirsty, as they seemed.

The third man was the one who was holding him.

"Well now," Yandor eyed him angrily, "you think you're pretty clever, don't you?"

Hanlon shrugged. "Doesn't look like it, does it?"

"Who are you spying for?"

"Who says I was spying?"

"Don't try to quibble with me, Gor Anlo. I want answers, and correct answers, or I'll let my pretty pets here take over, and see if you can elude them."

"And after I get through answering you'll cinder me anyway," Hanlon sneered. "Whatever gave you the idea I'd talk—if I had anything to say, that is?"

The mobster holding him cuffed him. "Don't talk to Ino Yandor that way, you phidi."

Hanlon turned his head and sneered into the man's face. "Watch who you're calling a snake." He twisted suddenly, drove his heel backwards into the man's shin, and pulled free. The fellow, even while yelping with pain, started to draw a flamer when Yandor commanded sharply, "Let him be. He can't outrun the tamous."

Hanlon spoke as though nothing had happened. "What gave you the idea I've been doing anything like you said?" he asked in a conversational tone. "What's this all about?"

"What were you doing, trying to look into—or get into—Adwal Irad's house?"

"That the name of the guy that owns it? Just looking for anything worthwhile I could pick up. I got to make a living someway since you got me fired just because I drank a little too much one night."

"Well now I hope you don't expect me to believe that. I know who you are, and my patience is at an end. Do you tell me who you are working for, and what you're after, or do I let the tamous loose?"

"I've got nothing to…" Hanlon began, but the man who had been holding him suddenly interrupted.

"Look, Yandor, at the man's ear!"

"Yes, and his feet," the other pointed downward.

They all stared closely, and Hanlon wondered as he saw their eyes widen. Then, with a start, he remembered kicking off his oversized shoes, and now he noticed that the dye had come off his hands. He guessed with sickening certainty that the long immersion in the saltwater had also loosened the plastic ears and nose, and that at least one of them had fallen off.

"By Zappa," Yandor stepped closer. "One of his ears is very small…" He reached out quickly and tugged at the other. Loosened at it was, it came off easily in his hand.

"An alien," Yandor exclaimed. "Your skin—it's not like ours."

"His nose seems false, too," the third man said.

Knowing his imposture was over, Hanlon himself pulled off the plastic overlay and disclosed his nose in its original size and shape.

"Yes, I'm a Terran. What're you going to do about it?"

"Loose the tamous!" Yandor snapped, and the man dropped the leashes he held.

But Hanlon had read that command in the impresario's mind even before he uttered it, and had already taken over the minds of the two beasts.

They were well equipped by nature to be deadly, even if that was not their true nature.

The female whirled, and jumped on the man who had been holding them. The male made two quick leaps, and was on the other gunman. Both men were borne backwards, and in seconds the great cat-things had torn out their throats.

"You should have remembered I'm the world's greatest animal trainer," Hanlon said evenly.

Yandor shrank back, sure he was next. "You fiend!" he cried, then his inherent cowardice showed and he threw himself on his knees. "Don't let them kill me," he pleaded in agonized tones. "I'll do anything—I'll give you everything I have. Only please, please keep those awful beasts away from me."

Hanlon hated a cowardly bully. Also, much as he detested killing or maiming, he had learned not to let it get him down too much in this work when it was necessary. But with such an unprincipled killer and abject wretch as the one before him, he felt no such compunction. He looked contemptuously down at the thing groveling at his feet in a very paroxysm of fear.

Disgusted, Hanlon turned away, climbed into the motor-trike in which Yandor and his men had come here, and started its engine. As he drove away he impressed a command on those now-slavering beasts, which then began bellying toward the helpless Yandor. But Hanlon could not repress a shudder of revulsion at what he felt forced to do.

After a half-mile or so of driving, however, the weariness, the pain and chill struck him, and he nearly fainted again. He struggled to keep himself conscious so he could get back home—a matter of vital necessity now that he was not disguised.

When he finally came to the more populated part of the city, in which people were beginning to be seen outside the houses and on the streets, he had himself fairly well under control. He kept his head down and made himself as inconspicuous as possible while driving at the highest allowable speed toward his rooming house. There he jumped from the car almost before it stopped, and ran in. He passed several of his neighbors in the hallways, but held his hand before his face and ignored their stares of surprise at his condition as he raced to his room.

Once inside, he locked the door, then breathed a sigh of deep relief. He began stripping off his wet and bedraggled clothes, thankful, as he remembered the loss of his shoes, that he had an extra pair of those specially made ones.

When he saw that much of the hair so meticulously glued onto his body was also coming loose, he thankfully ripped the rest of it from him, then went in and turned on the shower—really only a stream of water from the end of a pipe. For nearly a quarter of an hour he stood under it, reveling in the first feeling of real cleanliness he had known since leaving Simonides, relieved as the warm water washed the salt from his wounds and pores.

Finally, having treated his burns and bruises, he put on a dressing gown to partially cover his nakedness, and sank into his comfortable chair. Then he let his mind review the happenings of the past night.

Hanlon was once more in a cockily jaunty mood. He had taken some terrific risks, had been in almost-fatal jeopardy several times, had had adventures and escapes no one would believe if he tried to tell them—except some of the few SS men who knew about his special talents, and dad, of course...

Dad! He had almost forgotten his father's predicament in the excitement of the night. Now, as he considered and concentrated on this problem, Hanlon began to realize—dimly, sketchily, and much against his will—that things were not at all right, as he had felt for the moment.

He tried to dodge that flickering thought, but it persisted, grew stronger, would not be denied. He finally was forced to consider it more thoroughly. And slowly it dawned upon him that he had not *won*—he had lost. He had smeared up the works, but good. His campaign was done, finished, kaput. He had put his foot in it, clear up to the sacroiliac.

Worse than that—far worse—he had undoubtedly gummed up this whole Estrellan business. Not only was his own work undone, but now the natives would know that the Terrans were here, just as that propaganda machine had said. Now it would be practically impossible to make them believe that the Terrans were *not* responsible for their crime wave—and all the other things said about them.

"Me and my big swelled head," he castigated himself furiously. "I oughta be horsewhipped."

Almost he cried. His body was, by turns, ice cold and feverish. He cringed mentally and physically.

Was there any way—any possible way—he could redeem himself? Could he publicly admit that he and he alone was to blame, that he was here entirely on his own initiative, because he wanted to see Estrella join the family of nations?

No, that was absurd. He wouldn't be believed. No one in their right mind would ever conceive that a young man like him would do such a thing without some backing—undoubtedly full Federation backing.

He would have to resign from the secret service. Or—he gasped—were its members allowed to resign? Admiral Rogers had said it was for life, once he got in.

"But he didn't guarantee how long my life would last," Hanlon grimaced.

Well, he drew himself up proudly, there was a way. He was not afraid to die.

"Whoa, now, wait a minute. Let's think this out. Death's no answer." For a new idea had just struck him. He forced the worry, the fear, the...the self-pity...from his mind, and settled down to consider this new concept. Maybe it wasn't as bad as he had thought, after all.

"Yandor and his goons were the only ones who knew I was a Terran, and they're dead," he thought. "So they can't tell on me. And no one else knows it. Maybe I can go ahead, just as I was."

He rose to get dressed. There was still his father's imprisonment to be taken care of—if possible. Hanlon was sure now that it was in that little stone house back of Irad's mansion that the admiral was being held prisoner.

A casual glance in the glass, and he was suddenly conscious of his appearance. Hey, he couldn't go out like this, in broad daylight. Not looking like a Terran.

Swiftly he considered the possibilities. He would have to disguise himself again enough to escape notice on the street. But he was no cosmetician...even if he had the dyes, the plastics...

He sank into his chair again, and thought seriously. But even while he was trying to think and plan, his worn, tired body—exhausted as it had never been before, and depleted of all strength—could bear no more. Without even realizing it, he sank parsecs deep into profound slumber.

Sometime during the day, without his knowing it, he must have gotten up and lain down on the bed, for it was there he finally awoke. The room was dark; only a small ray of light came in obliquely through the window, from a distant streetlight.

He got up, wincing at his lameness and stiffness. He went through some calisthenics to take the soreness from his body, then washed, dressed, and prepared and ate something. He hunted through his duffel bag and found a pair of gloves to cover his hands. Before putting them on, however, he wound a scarf about his head and face, covering most of it except his eyes. He pulled his hat well down, then put on the gloves.

Leaving his room, he went inconspicuously along the darkest parts of the streets until he came to the marketplace and a certain stall that specialized in theatrical costumes and makeup. It was the same place where he had bought that roch-mask.

Walking purposefully, as though he had legitimate business there, he went to the rear of the shop. It was not too hard to break in and crawl inside. There, using his utmost care not to be discovered, he hunted about among the shelves until he found some facial putty, skin dyes, and other articles he needed. He left a couple of gold pentas on the counter in payment.

Then, just as cautiously, he retraced his way to his rooms.

CHAPTER FOURTEEN

THE NEXT MORNING WHEN SSM GEORGE Hanlon awoke, his first thought was one of concern for his father. An impatient, driving urge for action seized him and made him jump out of bed. Then logic and clear thinking came to the fore, although it required conscious effort for him to prepare and eat his breakfast first of all.

Hurriedly finished, though, he set to work on his new makeup, doing his level best to keep his thoughts on the difficult task at hand.

He had let his whiskers and hair grow from the time he first received this assignment, of course, so was not too much concerned about the hairiness he must present to the world when dressed. Luckily, although it had often been a source of annoyance—he was one of those men whose beard grows clear down his face and neck to join, with hardly a break, the hair on his chest. As for the body hair that had been so painstakingly glued onto his body before, he decided not to attempt that. He had not yet had to disrobe in front of anyone here; he was certain he would be able to avoid doing so in the future.

He rubbed liquid rouge, of a dark shade, well into the skin of his face, neck, hands and high up on his wrists, which took care of his coloring.

His main worry was the nose and ears, especially the nose. That would be most quickly noticed if it looked artificial. His first few attempts were not only badly done, but almost ludicrous. His usually fine muscular coordination seemed to be lacking. But he persevered and finally, after several hours, managed to mold a fairly reasonable snout and to so blend its edges into the skin of his face adjoining that it would, he felt sure, pass muster on casual inspection.

He built up his ears in like manner, but to help with this deception, in case of any close scrutiny, he covered them with a head bandage. He put his hat on, pulled it well down in front and on the sides, then examined himself critically in the mirror.

"Boy, that's a sloppy job, and how," he exclaimed, disgusted with his handiwork. "Trevor would disown me if he could see it." But he finally decided it would do…he hoped.

Now that he had finished he discovered he was sweating like a nervous caval. He held out his shaking hands, and looked at them critically. What, in John's name, was wrong with him, anyway?

And a thought he had, perhaps subconsciously, pushed far down into the furthest recesses of his mind, swept over him with full force.

He did not want to think that thought. More, he did not want to have to make that decision. But...

Manning was dead.

Hooper was fleeing insanely, perhaps also dead by now.

His father was captive, imprisoned, tortured...if still alive.

Only he, Hanlon, of the four, was left.

And he was...alone.

Again to his mind came his father's earnest and incisive statement, that getting Estrella to accept membership in the Federation was the most important thing that had come up in ages. It *had* to be accomplished, and quickly.

Deep down Hanlon knew what that meant. Individuals were expendable—the plan was not.

He was beginning to learn that while plans may blow up in one's face—as now—such happenings must be accepted philosophically, without too much backward longing, without too great remorse, and certainly—which was the hardest to accept—without letting personal feelings or sympathy for those lost or in danger keep the one or ones remaining from going ahead with new attempts to bring the mission to a successful conclusion.

For a long time Hanlon sat there. Resolutely now, he put his father out of his mind, and concentrated only on how he was to accomplish the task that confronted him—alone.

Finally he began to look at the larger aspects of the problem, to realize that he must quit hunting for individual criminals and possible members of the opposition, and work from the other end—the top.

"After all," he thought, "it is the Ruler who makes the decisions. Perhaps...no, I *must* go to work on him. I've got enough dope now as to who is behind this intrigue. Now I must reach Elus Amir himself, and swing him our way. But, in Snyder's name, how am I going to get to him?"

Plan after possible plan he discarded. He could not go to Amir as a Terran. In the first place, his word would have no weight. In the second place, he would undoubtedly have considerable trouble making the approach to the Ruler, if it was possible at all.

No, he would have to get close to him as a native. And to do that, he first had to know more—a lot more—about the Ruler as a man, his habits and usual daily routine.

Hanlon left the house and went to a number of places where men ate or drank, both for information, and to try out his new disguise. The latter must have been better than he thought, for no one seemed to notice. And in each place he visited, while eating or sipping his mild drink, Hanlon asked one or two discreet questions. None of these, by themselves, seemed to mean anything. But the answers, put together as Hanlon did when he returned to his rooms, gave him a fairly detailed picture.

He knew now that the Ruler stuck quite closely to his residence ("palace," Hanlon thought of it) although occasionally his duties took him to other cities on either continent, and sometimes he went out for an evening at the theatre, as he had done on Hanlon's opening night.

Otherwise, he was a hard worker, an excellent and well-loved Ruler, always studying carefully all suggested legislation that was presented for his consideration, always thinking of ways to better the condition of his people.

But to one thing he had learned, Hanlon gave the most consideration at the moment. Elus Amir, he found, went out almost every day for a ride on his caval, and usually along the same route. Hanlon knew what road that was.

Accustomed as he now was to thinking more in terms of animals than of men, the natural thought for Hanlon was to wonder how he could meet or study the Ruler through his caval.

The next day, therefore, the SS man rode out into the country, and posted himself at a convenient spot where he could watch without attracting too much attention, yet could see for several miles. He took one of the wheels off his motor-tricycle and unmounted the tire. This was to be his excuse for being so handy at the time of his planned meeting with the Ruler.

But something apparently changed Elus Amir's habits, for he did not ride that road that day. Ruefully doing a bit of under-breath griping, Hanlon replaced tire and wheel, then rode back toward town.

But after he had gone part way through the city streets, he thought of something else that must be done, and headed towards the place Morris Manning had found rooms.

Luckily, no one else had moved in, and no one appeared in the hall when Hanlon came back, after a quick trip to a tool stall in the market place, where he was able to buy a hacksaw. For Manning, as did the other SS men, had attached a hasp and pickproof padlock to his door. The Estrellans locks were ingenious, but could quite easily be unfastened even without the key.

These locks consisted of a metal rod, like a sliding bolt, which ran inside the wood of the door. There was a slip in the wood on either side of the door through which a key, inserted in the rod, could move it forth or back. When the bolt was moved into position with one end seated in the holder in the doorjamb, a turn of the key opened flanges on the rod that fitted vertically into prepared slots.

But a little patience easily enabled one who wished to get in, to trip those flanges with almost any small, flat-pointed instrument, even a penknife blade.

Now Hanlon cut through the hasp, evidently without attracting anyone's attention, for none of the neighbors came out to investigate the strange sounds. Inside Manning's room, he went about the sad business of collecting the dead secret serviceman's gear and belongings, to be sent back home on the sneakboat.

As he was cleaning out one of the chests, however, Hanlon discovered a small notebook he knew was of Estrellan make. He opened it idly, and found it was filled with native writing.

Excited now, for he was sure Manning would have written in Terran or I-S C code if it had been his work, Hanlon slowly began deciphering the words.

"Yow, this is hot stuff," he exclaimed after less than a page. "Wonder where Morrie got this? From Esbor's office or home, I'll bet."

He stuffed the book into his pocket for later study. He packed the balance of Manning's things, then left, mounted his trike and rode back to his own rooms.

All the balance of the afternoon and evening he worked at the translation of the entries in that book. It was, he found with great glee, a list of the names of various criminals who had been working under Esbor, and brief details of their various activities, as well as many other notes of similar nature.

One recent item caused a brief exclamation. "Ran Auldin came seeking a safe hiding place today," he read. "It having already been decided by Adwal Irad that the man's usefulness was over, he was cindered."

"Dirty killers," Hanlon growled, his brief moment of joy at the direct mention of Irad dimmed by the import of that entry. "No conscience whatever."

All in all, however, he was vastly pleased, and grew more so as he continued translating. For there were several mentions of Adwal Irad, and always pointing to him as the top man. Now he had real evidence of what he had believed—that this crime wave was directed by the Second-in-Line. Hanlon was vastly relieved.

In the morning, as he was preparing to go out again to see if he could contact Amir, a thought sent him to the mirror, attempting some changes in his makeup. He worked subtly and soon made himself look considerably older—about middle-aged. This, he felt, would make the Ruler listen more carefully to his evidence than he might to a younger man. Then he rode out to that country road.

Sometime later he saw Elus Amir riding that way. From Hanlon's vantagepoint he saw the Ruler and a single groom on their mounts while they were still some distance away.

Hanlon's mind reached out and touched that of the Ruler's steed. There were a few moments of anxious trying, and then he was in full control of the animal's mind. Through its eyes Hanlon looked out carefully along the road. It seemed fairly smooth, and he felt sure that if Amir was at all a good cavalman—as he must be after riding nearly every day—he would be able to stay in the saddle safely during the wild ride planned.

Hanlon made the beast suddenly snort and shy to one side, then break into a wild gallop straight down the road, despite the Ruler's frantic efforts at control.

Swiftly the caval pounded down the road, Amir working desperately to control it, yet seeming not to be too frightened by the runaway. The groom kicked up his own mount, but was hopelessly outdistanced.

Meanwhile the caval, controlled by Hanlon's mind within its own, paid no attention to the sawings and pullings on rein and bit, and continued its apparently frightened bolt.

As they neared the place where Hanlon was working on his machine, the young man straightened, looked, then jumped into the road. He started trotting toward them, waving his arms in an effort to make the caval stop its mad rush. But, although he let the animal slow somewhat, it kept running wildly.

As it drew closer, Hanlon moved a bit to one side, but still in the road. When the horse and rider were almost upon him he turned his back to them and started running in the same direction, looking back across his shoulder. Just as the caval came abreast, Hanlon suddenly leaped toward it, and grasped the bridle. At the same time his mind calmed that of the beast, and commanded it to slow and stop.

To the Ruler, Hanlon seemed to be dragged for several yards, still holding grimly to the reins he had grasped. When he finally brought the caval to a stop, it stood with heaving flanks and blowing nostrils.

"Whew," Elus Amir wiped his face, "that was fine work, my man. Many thanks. I don't know what got into the stupid beast. It has never done that before."

"Something must have frightened it," Hanlon said. He pretended he did not know who the rider was, having considered this point carefully. "Sure you can handle it now?"

"Yes, I think there'll be no more trouble. By the way, is there anything I can do to show my gratitude?"

Hanlon looked surprised. "Why I didn't do anything special. Couldn't let you get hurt."

The Ruler gazed at him peculiarly. "Don't you know who I am?"

"No, should I?"

"I am Elus Amir."

"Oh!" Hanlon made himself look properly surprised, then bent his knee in the Estrellan salute to the Ruler. "I beg your pardon, k'nyer, if I've spoken wrongly, for I did not know."

Amir smiled. "Well now that you do, I ask again, is there anything I can do for you? You must want something."

Hanlon shook his head. "Thank you, sire, but I wouldn't dream of imposing on your generosity. I'm sure I can find a job somewhere."

"Oh, you're looking for work?"

"Yes, k'nyer. I only recently came here from Lura."

"What can you do?"

Another shrug. "Farm work, tending animals, that sort of thing. I love animals, especially cavals. I'd hoped to get a job as stableman on one of the estates here."

The Ruler looked at his groom who had come galloping up, relieved to see that his master was unharmed, glancing curiously at this stranger who had saved the Ruler, and with whom he could see Amir had been talking.

"Are there any vacancies in our stable-force, Endar?" the Ruler asked.

"Why...why, no, k'nyer, not at present."

"Make one then," snapped Amir. "I want to give this man a good position. He is to take care of my personal string of cavals."

"As you order, sire."

"I don't like to make trouble for anyone, k'nyer." Hanlon protested. "I don't want a job if it means putting someone else out of work."

The Ruler's eyes lighted up with a friendly smile. "I assure you it won't. I like your attitude, my man. It is good to find someone who thinks of others before himself."

Once more Hanlon shrugged deprecatingly. "I've found in my lifetime, k'nyer, that it doesn't hurt me any to think of the other fellow. And the best part of it is, I've also found, that when I do so think unselfishly I always receive far more happiness than otherwise."

"Ah, a philosopher. I must have many talks with you. Can you get to the Residence all right?"

"Yes, sire, as soon as I finish fixing my tire."

"Report to Endar here, then, when you get there. I'll instruct him as we ride back."

"My thanks, k'nyer. I promise to serve you well and faithfully."

The Ruler nodded briefly and rode away, the groom following at a respectful distance. Hanlon hurriedly replaced tire and wheel, then rode off toward the palace. Watching through the caval's eyes, he timed it so he rode into the courtyard just behind the Ruler and groom.

Elus Amir was cordial as he dismounted. "I see you got here all right...by the way, you never told me your name."

"I am called Ergo Lona, k'nyer."

"All right, Lona. Endar, see that this man has good quarters and whatever clothing he needs. Introduce him to the work."

"As you order, sire." The two men bent their knees, then led the cavals to the stables as the Ruler went up the steps into the residence.

Hanlon noticed the groom was inclined to be a bit surly, and deduced the man was afraid of his job. He determined to make friends, if possible. It would hamper his work of spying if he had to watch for enemies close to him, like this man could be.

"Please tell me how I may help, Endar," he made his voice cordial, yet with a touch of servility. "I'm proud that our Ruler has given me work. I assure you I want to do everything to make good here. I know you must be important here, to be allowed to ride with K'nyer Amir, and I hope you will teach me the regulations. I realize I can never be anything but a stable helper, but I do want to be a good one. I hope we can become good friends."

The man unbent a little. "All right. I'll show you around."

They stabled the cavals and then the groom led Hanlon to a nearby building. It was of stone construction, five-sided, surrounded by flowerbeds and trees. It was not only harmonious with the palace and other buildings and grounds, but a pretty little house by itself.

"These are the living quarters for the grooms," Endar said as they mounted the steps. Inside he pointed out the dining room, then led the way upstairs and down a short hall. "This will be your room," he opened a door, disclosing a small but well-furnished, comfortable room.

"I have a few things in Stearra," Hanlon said. "When will it be convenient for me to go get them?"

"We have lunch in a few minutes, then you might as well go," Endar said. "I'll give you a note to the official tailor, and have him fit you with the proper clothes."

Hanlon looked at him as though with new respect. "Oh you must be the head groom then, nyer. I hadn't thought about that. Please pardon my presumption in suggesting that we be friends."

Endar merely looked at him a moment, then turned and left without a word.

Hanlon grinned to himself as the door closed. "It won't be too hard to keep ahead of that guy. Only I'll have to watch him all the time, or he could get nasty."

CHAPTER FIFTEEN

HANLON WAS AWAKENED SHORTLY AFTER dawn the next morning. "Darn this having to pretend to such jobs," he growled to himself as he rose, washed and dressed. He had always preferred to sleep as late as possible, and getting up at such ungodly hours did not tend to make him too happy the first few hours of the day. Yet, young as he was, he had developed the philosophy of accepting what must be as gracefully as possible, and now consoled himself with the hope that he would probably not have to keep up this imposture very many days.

His first care was to examine minutely, in the mirror, the makeup he had applied. The ears and nose still seemed to be all right and holding tightly. But he was careful, when no one was around during the days that followed, to look at them as often as he could in a pocket mirror he carried.

After a good breakfast in the dining room he was put to work cleaning, feeding and watering the cavals. Endar brought two of the horses from their stalls, snapped their halters into rings in a post, and was busy currying them. When he finished he saddled the two and led them out, after first telling Hanlon to make sure the stables were clean, in case the Ruler came to inspect them.

There were three other stablemen, working at the same general tasks. Hanlon, without neglecting his own work, made it a point to try to engage them in conversation.

"I love this kind of work, don't you?" he asked confidingly. "I'm so proud the Ruler gave me this job."

All the time he was studying their surface minds, trying to get a line on what manner of men they were—whether they would be inclined to be too friendly and intruding. But to his relief, he found they were rather stupid, loutish fellows, not caring too greatly what they did nor who was working with them, as long as they had a good place to live, plenty to eat, and fair pay. They seemed mildly surprised at his evident enthusiasm. One of them answered, in a churlish voice, "It's only a job—why get so excited about it?"

His mind-probings told him, however, that none of them was the type to be involved in any plot that might be going on, even as the most humble participants or workers. He had nothing to fear from them in any way.

When the work was finished for the morning, the other three men went into the tackroom and began playing cards. They ignored Hanlon, not asking him to play with them, seemingly not caring what he did.

He went outside, sought the shade of a large flowertree, and sat down with his back leaning against the bole. He closed his eyes, the better to concentrate, and strengthened his mental control of the cavals ridden by Elus Amir and Endar, in which he had put a smallish portion of his mind when they started out. He knew that so far no untoward incident had occurred—the Ruler was riding along that country road, wrapped in thought, not talking, not meeting anyone, paying no attention to the groom following him.

Hanlon had not expected anything would occur, but wanted to know if it did, and especially wanting to be sure he could perfectly control the Ruler's caval at all times, no matter what the distance.

Early the next morning a houseman approached the stables. "K'nyer Amir says to get his son's caval ready, for he rides with him today."

Endar indicated a certain animal to Hanlon. "Bring that one out and get it saddled. The young man's gear is the second set on the right of the door in the tack room."

Hanlon hurriedly led the caval out, snapped its halter ring in a nearby post, then ran to get the blanket, saddle and bridle.

"Those back legs aren't smooth," the head groom snapped. "Curry and brush them again. Inver is particular."

"Yes, nyer, thank you," Hanlon made haste to obey, and was careful in his work. When the beasts were ready, the groom took the reins in his hands, and led them to the mounting block.

Hanlon implanted parts of his mind in each of the two cavals. Thus he was ready for his spying when the two men came out of the residence.

Through the eyes, wide set in the only slightly elongated, broad heads of the steeds, Hanlon studied this important new character, of whom he had heard much. He saw a tallish, very intelligent-looking native, guessed him to be in his middle or late twenties. The fellow had a slight though wiry build, and reddish-blond hair and trimmed beard. Hanlon liked this Inver on sight, and decided instantly that what he had heard was somehow wrong. The Ruler's son certainly did not look half-crazy.

He pondered the matter. Was that impression being sowed about the planet deliberately? Was someone trying to tear down any reputation or influence the young man might have?

"This," his eyes gleamed, "is going to be good. I'm sure going to watch and listen carefully today."

Hanlon crowded into the brains of the two cavals all of his mind they could hold, finding that the animals had enough capacity to take a full half of his own mind. He had barely enough left in his body to keep on with his work which, luckily, did not require much mental effort. He still had more left than the other stablemen possessed.

The riders had barely left the palace grounds when Hanlon, through the caval's ears, heard the young man speak.

"I hope, father, that you have thought about the subject I broached to you the other day, and the reasons I suggested for your further study. I pray you have decided that our world will do well to join the Federation of Planets, as we have been invited to do."

Hanlon could tell by the tone, that the Ruler's mind and voice were troubled. "Son, I don't know what to decide. There are so many things to think about. There are many good reasons why we should…it is true. There are also many equally good reasons why we should not. I am, as you know, very jealous of Estrella's independence. I should hate to see it made subservient to any other power."

"But, father," Inver said earnestly, "we would not be. I have studied very carefully the proposition made us by the Federation Council, and the copy of their constitution they sent with it. They guarantee each planet complete autonomy, and state very plainly that the Council is only a judicial body set up to negotiate intra-planetary treaties and to see that the various worlds remain in harmony with each other. The advantages…"

"But it's all a trick of those Terrans to get control of the entire galaxy," his father broke in.

"That's not only nonsense, father, but a deliberate lie. I'm sure you know who is fostering it, and I think you can guess the reason."

"I presume you're still talking about the Second-in-Line. But Irad isn't like that, at all. He has a good mind, and he has presented some excellent reasons and arguments as to why we should not join the Federation."

"Sure, he would. He wants to keep Estrella free, so that when he takes over he can pluck it like a…"

"That's a strong indictment, son. I hope it is not jealousy because he won out over you in the tests."

"It is not jealousy, and while I haven't the proof yet, k'nyer, I do know it's true," the young man said hotly. "You can be sure that when I do get the truth I shall call for Irad's impeachment. No, father, I and many friends are concerned over this matter, and are satisfied we are correct."

Hanlon could guess at the trembled eyes of the older man, and that he was shaking his head sadly. "I hate to think that of Adwal Irad," he said. "He has always seemed so interested in helping me to build up Estrella's economy and is constantly bringing new ideas for her betterment. He seems to be making every effort to become worthy of his post when he succeeds me."

"I know," sadly. "He wasn't like this until recently. But he has changed someway, father. Now he is power mad. Also, he is trying to make me out as a fool and a brainless dara," Inver snapped.

"Why…why…I never heard him say anything like that," there was astonishment in the elder's voice. "He always speaks well of you."

"Naturally, k'nyer, he wouldn't be crass enough to say anything of that sort to you. But he and his henchmen are spreading that story all over our world."

"Oh I'm sure you must be mistaken."

"I'm not," grimly. "The evidence on that is unmistakable."

There was decisiveness now in the Ruler's voice. "If that's true I'll certainly put a stop to it."

"Don't, father, not at once," his son pleaded quickly. "Do not even mention it to Adwal yet, please. Nor make a public pronouncement about it. That would put him on his guard, and I and my friends need time to prove the other things I'm talking about."

"I'll not have word spread that my son is a…a weakling, or stupid," the elder's voice was angry, and Hanlon felt the jerk on the reins of his caval that told of the sudden gesture.

"Just so you don't believe it, father, is all I care at the moment."

Hanlon felt the two animals swerve and touch sides, and knew that Amir had drawn closer to his son, and shrewdly guessed he was touching the boy lovingly.

"You need never fear that, Inver. I've always been proud of the way you've taken hold of things, ever since you were a boy."

"I've tried, k'nyer, to make myself a worthy son of a great father," there was emotion in the young man's voice. "I've studied everything I thought would help me—economics, psychology, statecraft, history, and all. And especially since the Federation first made contact with us, I've tried to learn all I could about them, their various forms of government, their history, and everything. That's why I'm so sure they mean us well, not harm."

"But we're not Terrans. We're just semi-civilized beasts in their eyes."

"Another of Adwal's dirty lies," Inver snapped. "If they felt that, would they have asked us to join them as a full-fledged world? No, they would have come here with a fleet of warships of space, and conquered us. They could have, easily, you know. They made no effort to hide the fact that they had such power from the ones who were taken on that inspection trip."

"No, we have no spaceships, and nothing that could stop one," his father admitted. "That's one of the things that has made me hesitate to decide against them—the fact that they have them but did not use them. On the other hand, if we decide not to join, how do we know they won't send their fleet here and…"

"Because they aren't that kind of people. Why, sire, in their history I learned that when the Terrans first started exploring space, one of their great men, named John Snyder, who seems to have had quite a lot of power at the time, promulgated a ruling that says, 'Man must never colonize any planet having inhabitants intelligent enough to show cultural activity and growth.' And that concept has never been broken, and is still in force."

"Why I never heard that."

"I told you, k'nyer, I have been studying them diligently, and so know much about them."

For the balance of their ride that morning, the two continued their discussion, and Hanlon—working through the ears of the two cavals—listened closely, and learned much.

The two were almost back to the residence when Inver's caval stepped into a hole, and stumbled badly. It wrenched its leg so it could barely stand on it. Inver immediately dismounted and examined the leg as best he could.

"It looks bad, father," he said after a minute or so. "I'll walk the rest of the way, and lead it slowly. It's not too far from here, so you go ahead if you wish."

"Well," slowly, "all right. I'll have the doctor meet you at the stables, and see if the beast can be healed. If not, it should be destroyed to save it pain."

"Yes. I know that would be best, although I dislike to think of it, for this is my favorite."

The Ruler cantered on, and the young man followed slowly, letting the caval hobble along at its own gait. When Inver finally reached the stables, he talked with the head groom, Endar, and with the animal physician, who arrived shortly afterwards.

"I'm not sure," was the doctor's statement after much studying. "I'll try to save it, but I don't know if such an injury will heal or not. The ligament seems to have been torn loose, and being inside the leg it is hard to get at it with medicine. See how badly it has swollen already."

The caval was put into its stall, and after treating it as best he could with the limited knowledge and techniques known, the doctor left.

Hanlon knew about the accident, of course, and had been keeping the caval from feeling too much of the pain. He made it a point to be standing near while the animal was being examined and treated, and was surprised at how little the doctor could do. The Estrellan veterinarian did not even apply hot or cold compresses, nor bandage the swollen leg in any way. Also, apparently, he did not know about hypodermics for injecting medicine into the injured parts.

Later in the afternoon, after their work was done and he had some free time, Hanlon thought more concisely about the matter. If he could help any, he would make a friend of Inver, he felt sure. More than ever he liked the young fellow, whom he decided was a real man in every respect.

But he must be careful not to give himself away—not to display knowledge Estrellans did not know.

Suddenly he recalled the shooting of the fish and what he had been able to do there. "I wonder if I can help this healing in any way, with my mind?" he pondered.

The other grooms, including Endar, had left the stables for the bunkhouse, so Hanlon was there alone. He sat down near the injured caval's stall, insinuated his mind into that of the animal, and began studying its brain, nerves and muscles. After considerable intensive study he found the way to make its muscles relax—he had already long since established a nerve block so that the caval felt no pain. Now he learned to make those muscles and nerves contract or relax, even to the point of almost causing a temporary paralysis.

Deeper and ever deeper he probed into its physical structure. Especially now, he tried to trace the nervous system connecting with its various glands, looking for confirmation or refutation of a startling concept he had glimpsed.

After much study and experimentation by the trial and error method, he was beginning to find it possible to partially control the increase or decrease of flow of the secretions of its glands— but far from perfectly. For it was an intricate and involved method, necessitating as it did the locating of the nerves that led to and controlled those glands, and then learning how to activate or inhibit them—nor could he be sure it was not chance only the few times he made them operate as he wished.

Yet he watched carefully to see the results of the activations of each gland, and finally believed he had found the one that was the master gland in charge of the body's healing functions. He now worked on this, trying to direct the added secretions through the blood stream and into the caval's injured parts.

Soon, even though his forcings were spasmodic and infrequent, he could begin to perceive that this was actually the way it should be done—the wounded ligaments and flesh and muscles showed signs of starting to heal a bit faster than nature was doing it.

His deep concentration was rudely broken by a heavy hand on his shoulder, and an angry voice saying, "What d'you think you're doing here?"

Looking up, he saw that it was Endar. Hanlon recalled the portion of his mind from that of the caval.

"Oh," he scrambled to his feet and fixed his face in a look of deep concern. "I was just studying Inver's poor caval, and trying to figure out a way to help cure its leg."

The head groom sneered. "I suppose you think you know more about it than I do, or the doctor."

Hanlon was certain he knew far more than the groom, and probably things the doctor had never even guessed. But he kept his voice humble and almost servile. "I didn't say or mean that, nyer. But I have had some experience with animals, as I told you and the Ruler, and I've helped cure many injured ones. Since it was my off time, I didn't think I was overstepping my place to see what I could do."

"You been handling it?" Endar asked sharply.

"Oh no, nyer, I was just sitting here thinking about it, and trying to remember all I had learned or heard about how such injuries have been healed. Then I was going to come and suggest them to you."

"Well, it's none of your business, so get out and leave it alone," was the surly command…and Hanlon left.

But that night, after he was sure the others were all sound asleep, he sent his mind back to the stables and into the brain of Inver's injured mount.

In its spaceship the strange being was feeling a depth of frustration almost unknown to one of its cold, logical race. Its "interrogation" of the prisoners had yielded surprising but already-deduced information. In its rational yet impersonal way the being was somewhat regretful for the death of the one entity. Not because of the death itself, but because there was no logical reason why the entity should be dead, and therefore unable to yield further data.

The one still remaining imprisoned had given up much additional knowledge of a kind that had shocked the being, for it told of conditions never before considered as obtaining in the galaxy. Yet the being did not see how that information could help in this present project—it was, in fact, decidedly inimical to that project's success.

As for the one that had been allowed to "escape," that one had led to the unreadable mind as hoped. Although still kept controlled and unsane, the being was allowing that one to remain in what it considered a safe hiding place, rather than continually on the run.

But even though the being had now been following that enigmatic entity's body, through its powerful, multiphased scanners, it still could not make any sort of contact with that mind. Thus it did not yet know whether or not that mind was like the other three, or the two that came occasionally and briefly in their ship of space. Under its easily penetrated disguise, the entity appeared to be like the others, but that could or could not mean anything worth knowing.

It was all very puzzling, and the alien being came as near feeling anger as was possible to one of its phlegmatic nature. But it coldly resolved that that one must, also, die…and soon.

CHAPTER SIXTEEN

DARKNESS MADE NO DIFFERENCE TO GEORGE Hanlon in dealing with animal minds for it was not with his eyes that he "saw" what was inside them. In this particular instance he was grateful for the dark—it made concentration far easier.

He made himself comfortable on his bed then fitted his mind to that of the wounded animal in the stable. Deeper and ever deeper he probed, tracing line and connectors and synapses carefully. A stray thought brought a grin to his face. "I bet I'm learning things no veterinarian ever learned about animals."

Then he sobered quickly. "Perhaps I should write this up for them—the physiology and endocrinology of it I mean." He filed the thought away in his mind for future reference. It would be a great contribution to those branches of science, he felt—*if* he was successful.

Now he traced nerves, blood vessels, cells, glands. He bored in with every newly awakened sense alert to catch each particle of new knowledge. He began to learn even more of how the healing and regeneration of cells and tissues worked…and after awhile he achieved real beginnings of success.

The things he had been able to do that afternoon with his first studies, had started the healing of the caval's leg somewhat faster than nature ordinarily did it, but not much more. Now, however, he was able more surely and quickly to continue that work, and by the time he noticed the false dawn lightening the night a bit, and he knew he must get some sleep, the injury was almost entirely healed.

"What a surprise Endar's going to get when he looks at that leg in the morning," he chuckled. For the swelling was reduced, the inflammation all gone, and the caval was able to stand and walk on the foot without limping or apparent pain. In fact, from his ability to read the beast's mind Hanlon knew the pain was all gone. If nothing happened to irritate it, the leg would be as good as new in a day or so without further attention.

Hanlon was sleeping so soundly the next morning that Endar had trouble waking him, and that did not help in dispelling the anger and distrust in him the head groom knew. Hanlon tried to work hard enough, and was careful to appear willing and ready even for the mean, dirty jobs Endar assigned him, so as not to make the groom any more irritated than he already was.

Shortly after daylight Inver came to the stables to see how his favorite caval was getting along. He and Endar were very much surprised to see that the animal was apparently entirely well, and that the leg showed no signs of the injury of the day before.

"I can't understand it," the young man shook his head. "It must not have been as badly hurt as we thought."

Endar may have had his doubts—and Hanlon saw him throw a quick, wondering glance in his direction—but the groom wisely said nothing, since he had no proof...and such a thought was ridiculous, anyway.

When it came time for the Ruler's morning ride, Hanlon was still working inside. But Elus Amir asked to see the new man and Endar had to call him out.

"Ah, my savior," Amir said as Hanlon appeared. "Are they treating you well, Lona?"

Hanlon bent the knee. "Oh yes, k'nyer. I have everything to make me happy here, and I love the work. And Endar has been most kind about showing me around, and helping me learn all my duties here so I may serve you better."

"Good. I'd like to have you ride with me this morning," the Ruler said as he mounted.

Hanlon glanced at Endar. He could see that the head groom was not pleased by this, though he said nothing, merely handing the reins of the second mount to Hanlon then turning away. Hanlon was quickly astride, and the two riders started off at a brisk canter.

As soon as they were well away from the residence Amir slowed down and motioned Hanlon to come to his side. "Now, tell me all about the Eastern Continent—what conditions are like there, and what the people are saying about things in general."

Hanlon dredged his mind for any and all information he could remember from his studies of the reels of Estrella furnished him by the secret service, as well as what he had learned from others since he came to this planet.

For nearly a penta-period he told what he knew, then said, "One thing is quite noticeable there, k'nyer. The ordinary people I talked to over there—of course I don't know any of the important ones—all seem very anxious for our world to join the Terran Federation of Planets."

"They are?" the Ruler seemed surprised, but interested. "I thought there was quite a bit of sentiment against it."

Hanlon shrugged as though it was of no importance. "Oh, you hear a lot of talk going around that we would lose our freedom, and that the people of the Federation just want to enslave us, but no one I talked to seemed really to believe it. They think someone there is putting out a lot of propaganda because of some personal reasons. The ordinary people think they would benefit greatly by such a union with more advanced people. One of our newssheets printed a copy of the Federation Agreement, and it states very clearly that all worlds are to have full right to choose their own form of government, and that they keep their full...their full..."

"Sovereignty," the Ruler supplied the missing word. "Thank you, k'nyer...their full sovereignty at all times. It also went on to say that all the other worlds do just as they please, and that the only purpose of the Federation is to encourage trade and the spread of knowledge among the various planets in an equitable way, and yet see to it that they never get into war with each other, by settling all possible disputes before they get to the explosive point."

Elus Amir was silent for long minutes, thinking seriously, and Hanlon followed those thoughts as they chased themselves across the screen of the Ruler's mind. Finally Amir raised his head. "er...yes, yes, that's all true enough, Lona. But if it is so, why is there such a seemingly determined effort to persuade me and the people here that it is not true?"

"May I speak my thoughts, k'nyer?"

"Eh? Why, of course," Amir looked up in surprise. "That's why I wanted you to come along today."

"Well, sire, it looks to me—and please remember that I'm just a simple countryman, and not used to politics or statesmanship—but it looks to me as though someone wanted to keep us by ourselves so they could run this world the way they want to, and be able to make themselves rich or powerful at the expense of our common people."

"But that's impossible as long as our government is on its guard."

"Exactly, k'nyer. It could not be done as long as you are Ruler, but suppose you..."

Elus Amir's head snapped up irritably at this unfinished warning. "The Second-in-Line is just as jealous of Estrella's welfare as I am," he snapped. "It would not happen under him either."

But Hanlon, reading the Ruler's surface thoughts, knew he must keep quiet for the moment. For Amir was disturbed by hearing this idea from a simple groom. He did not want to give it credence, but doubt had been forced into his mind, first by his son, and now by this man.

But before he could formulate any decisive answer, Hanlon decided boldly to jolt him again.

"I have a friend, k'nyer," he reached into his inner pocket and brought out some papers, "who has been actively studying this matter for some time. He has found out a number of things I am sure will interest you, and about which I doubt very much you know."

The Ruler looked at him sharply. "What do you mean?"

"You know that there has been an unprecedented crime wave all over our planet recently," Hanlon said, and Amir nodded sorrowfully. "My friend has found proof that, while a lot of people have been engaged in those criminal activities, there is a complete program that is being carefully carried on by a staff of head men, each with his own group of lower criminals, but all headed by one…"

"By the Terrans—it is well known here."

"No, k'nyer, not by the Terrans. The real leader of this campaign of destruction is the same man who is the leader of the opposition to Estrella's joining the Federation."

"And that man?" the Ruler snapped, but his face was drawn, as though he already knew…but would not let himself believe.

"That leader, k'nyer, is Adwal Irad."

"Prove it, or by Zappa I'll have you executed," Amir's voice crackled. "Have a care, Lona, and don't try my patience. I don't allow myself to be talked to in that manner."

"I crave pardon, sire, if I have spoken out of line. But you asked me for my reactions and knowledge, and I must be truthful."

"Whatever gave you such foolish notions? And who are you, anyway? A countryman such as you claim to be would not know about such things or use such precise language."

"You might be surprised, k'nyer, if you knew how many of your humbler subjects are vastly interested in the welfare of our world, and who read and think much about these things, even though they know they cannot fully understand them. As to how I got such ideas, the answer is many things. And facts collected by my friend. Including this little book," handing him Esbor's notebook, "which was found in…well, in a certain place.

It contains a lot of information we were sure you would want to study, which is the reason he asked me to give it to you if I got the chance."

The Ruler took the book, opened and glanced through it. Hanlon could see the start of surprise he made, and read the thoughts that flashed through the Ruler's mind as he saw some of the notations. During the remainder of the ride, now at a slow walk, there was complete silence, until they were nearing the residence's courtyard. Then Amir looked at Hanlon, a shrewd look on his face.

"You're a curious fellow, Lona. Who are you, really?"

"One of the many who have the interests of yourself and this world very much at heart," Hanlon said honestly. "Please do not ask me more, but believe that we are honest and sincere. Your son has many friends..." He stopped, letting it go at that, knowing the Ruler's memory would flash back to the talk with Inver the day before, and hoping Amir would not pursue his questioning.

Elus Amir began studying Hanlon closely—an examination the young man knew might quickly disclose his imposture. He made his caval suddenly shy away, and took several moments controlling it enough so he could ride back to the Ruler's side— but stayed a bit further behind than he had been before.

As he had hoped, this maneuver had given Amir time to think. "Very well," the Ruler said, "I'll not inquire too closely at the moment, although you may be sure..." His voice became more stern now. "...that I shall be on my guard to know if you are really working for me or not."

He was silent a moment, then added slowly, "But as to what you have said, and this book...well I promise to study them thoroughly."

Hanlon thanked Elus Amir for his courtesy to a humble groom. "And thank you for the great privilege of riding with you, and talking to you. I have always felt, k'nyer..." He made bold to add, "...that we have a truly great Ruler. Now..." He smiled sincerely. "...I am more sure of it than ever."

"Why, thank you, Lona. I do try to watch out for the best interests of our people."

"A groom should not presume to advise his Ruler but I feel emboldened to say that your people would be glad if you decide to join the Terran Federation," Hanlon said humbly, then added more earnestly, "and I beg you, sire, watch out for yourself. There are human tamous aboard."

The Ruler looked startled, but said nothing to this although he became very thoughtful as he left. Hanlon, except for one point, was well content with his morning's work as he led the cavals back to the stable.

For Hanlon had so much wanted to tell Amir how he could know for a certainty who among his attendants and guards was really trustworthy, but did not dare mention it at this time. It would have been fairly easy for Hanlon to be inconspicuously present—perhaps hidden by a screen—while the Ruler called his guards and servants in one by one and questioned them. For Hanlon could then have read their minds or surface thoughts, and undoubtedly have been able to tell which ones, if any, were lying. But to have even mentioned such a thing would have been to reveal too much that he was not yet ready to have known.

"I'll have to hang around the guards as much as possible, and study their minds for any traitorous thoughts," he decided. "I especially want to know if any of them are Irad's tools."

Endar was surly when Hanlon brought the mounts into the stable, although he did nothing overt as the young man carefully rubbed down the cavals, and returned them to their stalls.

But Endar did come up then and ask, "What did Amir have to talk to you about?"

"We did very little talking," Hanlon answered with apparent truthfulness. "He asked me a few questions about Lura and the Eastern Continent, but I told him I was just a farm worker and didn't know much about general conditions. That seemed to disappoint him, and he said nothing more."

"But I saw him talking to you as he dismounted, and you were answering him."

"Yes, he was kind enough to say he enjoyed the ride, and that the cavals were in fine condition. I told him that was largely due to you, that you were careful to see that they were well cared for, and that we kept the stables clean."

"That reminds me, how did it happen that Inver's caval was all healed this morning?" the man's eyes bored suspiciously into Hanlon's.

"Why I don't know," he answered evasively, his face bland. "I suppose it was the medicine and treatment the doctor gave it. He must really be good—but then, he wouldn't be the Ruler's animal physician if he wasn't, would he?"

"Humph." Endar swung away, but his attitude and surface thoughts told Hanlon that he was only partially satisfied. He had no real idea, of course, of what had happened. Such a thing was just beyond his simple comprehension.

George Hanlon could not know it, of course, but as soon as the Ruler had returned to his rooms, he settled himself comfortably in his favorite chair, and gave orders that he was not to be disturbed. Then he set his mind to considering every aspect of this curious business, and to studying more thoroughly the papers and that notebook of Esbor's, with its disquieting notations.

Finally he called in the man who was not only a sort of confidential secretary, but a lifelong friend and confidant whom he trusted implicitly. He gave this man definite orders as to certain investigations to be made at once.

During the balance of the day, while this man was gone, Amir's mind was a turmoil of doubt. And worry—for Hanlon's final suggestion that the Ruler's life was in great danger, made him pause to think. Of course, Rulers were always fair targets for assassins, even on this world where such things were very rare, indeed. But...Lona had hinted that this was no ordinary assassination he was to watch out for, but a part of the so-called "plot" of a group who were out to keep Estrella from joining the Terran-led Federation.

And if the groom was right, then how safe was Amir? Even in his own residence…was his personal guard loyal? Or had the conspirators…supposing there was such a group…?

The Ruler was still reluctant to believe Irad was at the head of any such organization, or even connected with it in any way, despite the mounting evidence…including more than one entry in Esbor's revealing notebook. Had these conspirators, whoever they might be, been able to infiltrate members into his hitherto highly trusted household? Wait, come to think of it, there were several new servants and guards, come to work there within the past half-year or so!

Elus Amir had never heard of truth serums, or lie detectors, for such things had not yet been discovered or invented on Estrella. Nor did he even suspect that it was possible to read a man's mind.

Now the Ruler's thoughts strayed back to that enigmatic groom. Just who and what was he, anyway? He certainly was not a common, simple countryman, as he pretended to be. And the way he had met the Ruler, saved his life, and had obtained work here. Looking back now Amir could see that it was all too pat.

Was he one of those "friends" Inver had spoken about, who were working with his son to find out the truth about whatever it was that was going on here? It was apparent he was part of a group of some kind, or else his talk of a "friend" who had obtained that damning notebook was false, and Lona himself had managed to get possession of it.

Acting on a sudden impulse, Amir sent a servant to ask Inver to come to see him. When the young man arrived, the Ruler looked at him a moment.

"Just one question, my son. Are some of those 'friends' you spoke to me about yesterday numbered among the residence servants or guards?"

Inver looked startled, but his reply was patently honest. "Yes, father. We have been checking the others carefully, and when we find those we distrust in the least, we manage to get them discharged, and others we can trust brought in to replace them. Why?"

But the Ruler did not answer that last. He merely said, "Thank you, Inver. That is all for the present."

Now the young man really was astonished at this abrupt dismissal, but left without further words.

Elus Amir felt better now. He had always considered himself a fairly good judge of character—although he was beginning to wonder now if all that was being told him about Irad was true, for if so, then he had made a bad mistake in judging the Second-in-Line, for he had always had full confidence in his integrity.

But about this Lona? He sent a servant to bring Endar, the head groom, to see him. When the man arrived, Amir asked him many questions as to what Endar thought of the new man. He realized almost from the first that Endar was jealous of Lona's popularity with the Ruler, but Endar produced no actual facts against the new stableman, and grudgingly had to admit that he was a good and willing worker.

Yes, Amir now decided, whatever else this Lona might be, he was a true patriot, trying to serve the best interests of his country and his Ruler in every way he could. There was a straight-forwardness about him that Amir liked, and evidently Inver also had confidence in him.

Yet there was a tantalizing *something* about Lona's looks that had the Ruler a bit puzzled, although it was more subconsciously than consciously.

For the time being, he decided, he would allow Lona to remain here. It would be easier to keep watch on him here than if he let him go and the groom should disappear entirely. Also, Amir determined to have further talks with this strange man...and with Inver, about the latter's "group of friends."

Finally, some time after dinner that evening, the Ruler's secretary came back to report. "I have examined the news records, k'nyer, and the first mention I can find of anything like propaganda against our world's accepting the invitation of the

Federation Council was printed in the Stearran papers about a week after the group returned from that trip made to visit the Terran planets."

"Hmmm, not until then, eh…but that seems to tally with some other things I've heard. Still, it is curious. Another point is still bothering me, and I'd like your thoughts on it. The Terrans evidently discovered us long before we knew it, and studied us even to the extent of learning our language, while still keeping us in ignorance of their existence. It was this apparent stealth that has led many of us to wonder if they are sincere, or if there is some underlying motive of conquest behind them. What do you think?"

"As you know, k'nyer," the secretary reached up to tug at his beard while thinking and replying, "I was permitted to be present at the meetings you had with the Federation representatives, and I was very much impressed with them. I have also talked much with those who went on the trip to the Terran planets. I cannot conceive the possibility that these Federationists are practicing duplicity. Besides, let us consider our own actions in such a case. Suppose we had space travel, and found a new world inhabited with intelligent beings. Would we not, if possible, study them thoroughly before trying to make contact with them?"

Elus Amir shrugged, and his answer was to the first part of his friend's speech. "That might depend upon how well they were able to conceal their true feelings—upon how good actors they were."

"Perhaps, but…"

"Never mind that for now. What about the rumors concerning my son, Inver?"

"Those were much harder to check, but in my own mind there is no recollection of ever having heard of any such thing until the past year. However, I have heard reports of it since, and it seems to be spreading rapidly all over."

"And you never reported this to me?"

The secretary hung his head. "I did not believe it, sire, and I didn't like to worry…"

"It's all right. So it was just about a year ago that the opposition to our joining the Federation appeared, and also these rumors."

"Why…why, yes, sire. Do you connect the two?"

Amir did not answer that last question. He sat very quietly as to body, but with mind active and ill at ease. After a bit he raised his eyes and asked suddenly, "Just what is your personal opinion of Adwal Irad. Speak freely—I want the truth."

The secretary's eyes clouded, but he did not hesitate. "I have noticed a great change in the Second-in-Line, growing more pronounced recently. As though something were preying on his mind. His actions have become…well, 'shifty' is the nearest word I can think of to describe it. I no longer trust him unreservedly I'm sorry to say."

"Hmmm," Amir thought about that for some time. "I have had the same thing told me by others these past few days," he said at last. "I wish I knew…"

"May I suggest, k'nyer, that you invite him to ride with you tomorrow, and study him; ask him leading questions, and so on?"

"That might not be a bad idea. I'll do it. Send him an invitation in my name, please."

After the note had been received, and while Irad was changing his plans so as to accept this command, he suddenly seemed to get a feeling that he must do a certain thing. The Second-in-Line recoiled in horror. He did not want to comply—did not even want to think such a thought. This was far worse than the other things he had been forced to do in the past months. But something…he could not imagine what or why…was forcing him to do this, as it had the others.

Reluctantly, fighting with all his will not to do what he somehow had to do, he sent word to several of his men and, when they arrived at his home, gave them explicit instructions. They seemed surprised, and reluctant, but he insisted and, somewhat to their surprise, the plan soon seemed like a good one.

CHAPTER SEVENTEEN

THE NEXT MORNING HANLON WAS TOLD TO take two cavals out to the mounting block, for Adwal Irad was to ride with the Ruler that day. As the two men came out of the residence and Hanlon got his first good look at the Second-in-Line for some time, he was thunderstruck at the man's appearance—it was so changed from when he had seen him the other times.

Irad's face was drawn and the red of his skin was an unhealthy hue. Deep lines were beginning to show in his face, the eyes were so dim and lack-luster, the mouth so drawn that Hanlon wondered if Irad was ill, or had been these past few days.

For the one who had passed highest in all his tests from among those eligible in his generation as to knowledge and fitness for the position of Second-in-Line, and successor to the Rulership, such a breakdown seemed incredible.

Hanlon invaded Irad's mind to see if he could learn why all this was. But at first touch there seemed something wrong with it…as though there was a block or barrier there in that mind unlike any he had ever before found. It seemed even worse than it had been before when he had tested that mind—and he wondered anew what it could possibly be. He could still read Irad's surface thoughts, but the "feel" of the man's mind was different and disturbing.

Hanlon's mind scanning, however, was just in time to catch the partial thought, "…this the fellow? He'll bear watching."

It was not much to go on, but Hanlon instantly became more alert. "What in Snyder's name does that mean?" he asked himself. "Wish I had some way of watching this bozo when he isn't around me."

But he did not know of any way it could be done, for he could not very well leave the palace grounds while he was working here as a groom, to spy in person upon Irad's coming and goings, and he knew of no animal or bird kept in the home of the Second-in-Line.

"Wonder what became of Ebony?" Hanlon thought parenthetically. "Hope he found a way to get out of Yandor's house, and that he has a new, good home."

And this brought up the sternly repressed memory of his father. Oh how he wanted to drop everything and go hunt for his dad. But he had already thought the matter through, and knew his duty kept him at his work—work that was far more important than one man's liberty. Yes, his mind knew that, but his heart did not.

But Hanlon could and did keep in touch with the two men through the minds of their cavals as they rode that morning, even as he returned to his work in the stables.

And it was well he did so. For hardly were they outside the gates when Irad began again to argue against Estrella's joining the Federation. But today his so-called evidence met stiffer opposition than formerly. For the Ruler had been thinking more seriously than before, and was studying what Irad said with that in mind.

The things Hanlon—as Lona, the groom—had said had been disturbing. At first Amir had been tempted to dismiss them as ridiculous, even though they more or less echoed what his own son, Inver, had told him. But that damning notebook and its entries was something the Ruler could not dismiss, nor the reports and comments of his lifelong friend and respected secretary. He was still undecided—but he was no longer to be duped by sincere-seeming words.

Now, as the two men rode along, Amir was remembering those things and judging each statement Irad made with what he had heard.

And SSM George Hanlon, "listening in" via the minds and senses of the two cavals he was controlling, shivered a bit in the distant stables. He felt a premonition…but could not deduce what, nor how, nor even if. But he determined to keep closer watch than ever, and so tightened his control of the two steeds cantering along that dusty road several miles away.

As he had found he was able to do, the portions of his mind in each of the animals was, in a large sense, complete and able to act of and by itself. Yet both portions were connected with each other, and with the balance of his mind in his own brain, by a thin thread of consciousness.

He had never quite gotten used to the sensation of apparently being in several places at the same time—of being several distinct individualities. He still remembered the thrill he had known when it was first demonstrated, and the times it had saved him. Yet it was a weird feeling, even though he had found how wonderfully it could and did help him in the important work assigned him by the secret service high command.

Only a few minutes later, however, he was glad he had the power. The Ruler and Irad were passing a small wood, when suddenly several other cavalmen came racing from it, and surrounded them. Two of the new men—all of whom were masked—caught the bridles of the two animals from the residence, and halted them abruptly.

"What is the meaning of this?" Elus Amir cried imperiously, apparently more angry than frightened.

But Hanlon, so far distant he could not possibly get to the place personally, in time to be of any help, was worried and scared. This attack had all the earmarks of assassination and, knowing what he knew, he was sure it was intended as such.

He must do something, but quick.

Dropping his pitchfork, he raced into the tackroom when he knew there was a cot. Throwing his body down on this, he sent all the remainder of his mind out to contact and control the cavals of the newcomers—working outward from the two he was already controlling that were at the scene.

He did not have mind enough to fully take over all of them at once, for cavals had potentially much mind-power, and four or five could absorb all his.

However, by temporarily dropping control of Amir's animal, he was able to take over enough regulation to overcome the commands of the riders. He made the horses of four of the assassins—those holding flameguns—rear back and begin fighting their riders. They pitched and bucked and shortly started dashing off on a wild runaway gallop across the meadow, in different directions. He impressed on each caval's mind as well as he could that it must keep on running, no matter what was done to stop it.

Then he wrenched control from their minds and sent it into the other four animals. He found he was just in time. One of the men, who had been holding Amir's caval (Hanlon could see through its eyes), was drawing his flamegun.

Hanlon made this caval rear suddenly, pitching the man off onto the road. The animal swiveled about while in the air and landed its heavy feet on the prone body. It kicked and pawed the helpless gangster until there was nothing left but a battered and bloody mass.

The remaining attacker's caval was, meanwhile, racing off across the meadow in much the same runaway fashion as the ones that had preceded it. When it was well away, Hanlon withdrew control.

Meanwhile, he had been watching carefully through the eyes and ears of the two steeds that bore the Ruler and the Second-in-Line, what they were doing and saying.

Through Irad's mount he could see the look of surprise and fright that had come upon the Ruler's face. Fright, Hanlon rightly guessed, at Amir's near approach to death, surprise that the attack had been made at all, and especially at the unbelievable manner of his deliverance.

"What could possibly have made all those cavals start running away just at the crucial moment?" he asked Irad, whom he did not yet suspect. "And even more amazing, the way that one threw and then so savagely killed its rider, yet is now standing quietly there, munching grass at the roadside?"

But both Amir, and Hanlon—who saw it through the Ruler's caval's eyes—saw the look of hatred and rage that came onto the face of the Second-in-Line, giving it almost the appearance of a completely different person. Amir was so shocked by it that for a moment he could not speak—could only stare in open-mouthed amazement. Hanlon too was startled, momentarily failing to watch the actions of Irad.

And in that instant the conspirator tried to act. From a hidden pocket in his clothing he drew a flamer, and aimed it at the Ruler.

"Maybe this will spoil my plans," he snarled, "but by Zappa, you die anyway."

But even as he was speaking, and while he was pressing the stud in the gun's handle, Hanlon snapped himself into awareness, and made Irad's mount rear back and wheel on its hind legs, while at the same time he forced the Ruler's caval to dodge to one side.

However, he was not quick enough. There was a flash of flame, a stench of burning cloth and flesh, and a hastily-suppressed groan, all clearly apparent through the cavals' senses that told the distant Hanlon that Amir had been hit. He felt the Ruler reel in his saddle, and hoped the blast was not fatal.

But he had no time then save for an incidental inspection, despite the abilities of his divided mind. For he was intent on trying to make Irad's caval unseat its rider, so that he might have the beast trample the conspirator. Even so he could feel Amir—through the senses of the steed the Ruler was riding—clutch the pommel with both hands to hold himself on his mount's back.

But Adwal Irad was an excellent cavalman. He managed to keep his seat, but was too busy with this either to look to see if his shot had killed his Ruler, or to fire another. In a moment he had to drop the gun, anyway, in order to use both hands in trying to quiet the raging animal beneath him.

For the caval was rearing, bucking, sun-fishing—every unusual maneuver Hanlon's agile mind was able to make it perform. It did things no caval, and no Estrellan, had ever heard of before. Through its mind Hanlon could feel the cruel whipping Irad was giving it, and this made both Hanlon and the beast—never more than half-tame at best—viciously angry and more determined than ever to get rid of the burden.

Realizing at last that he could not unseat so skillful a rider, Hanlon changed his tactics. He made the caval start off on a dead run—but into the woods, not across the meadow as the others had done. "Maybe it will run under a low branch and knock Irad off his back," he hoped.

But he was worried about Amir, and turned most of his mind back to seeing how the Ruler was faring. He knew the man was still astride, and with part of his mind he could read pain, but knew Amir was not fatally injured. Hanlon made his mount turn back toward the residence, and at its gentlest speed hasten back until he saw the servants come running out to take care of their master.

Knowing the Ruler was now in safe hands, Hanlon was free to think of his own situation.

He opened his eyes...and stared with growing astonishment at totally unfamiliar surroundings.

Jerkily he sat up on the bunk on which his body was now lying. His eyes roved about the small, stone-walled room, trying to figure out where he was...and why.

He had gone into the familiar tack room of the stables, he knew, to lie down on the cot there while he sent all of his mind out of his body to contact and control the cavals of the would-be assassins. He guessed he had been "gone" for about half an hour. What had happened in the meantime?

He got up and went across the small room to a heavy wooden door, which he found to be locked. He had to stand on tiptoes to look through the small, barred window in it. But his only view was of a narrow corridor, on the other side of which was another stone wall containing, in the limited portions he could see to either side, three doors similar to the one behind which he was confined.

"Looks like I'm in the *juzgado,*" he grimaced. "Wonder why, and how?"

He called out, in hopes someone would come and explain. But repeated calls brought no one, nor any response from the other cells. "Must be no one else here," he thought, and went back to lie down on the bunk.

There he used his special talents, sending his mind outside and hunting for some bird or animal through whose eyes he could try to discover where he was.

He finally contacted a bird, and soon discovered he was in a small stone building at one of the farther corners of the residential grounds. There did not seem to be any guards hanging about the outside. Hanlon made the bird fly up and hover near one of the windows, and peer inside. No one there, either. Nor any to be seen through either of the other windows that opened to the outer wall.

He sent the bird higher until he could see the entire palace grounds and thus orient himself. Then he flew it to the stables.

Endar was talking to two other grooms, and seemed in high spirits. As the bird found a perch close to the little group he heard Endar saying, "...drunk, so I had the guards arrest him."

"Never knew he drank," one of the stablemen said.

"I was surprised, myself, but he was dead to the world, and I couldn't rouse him."

But Hanlon could detect, in the man's voice and attitude, that Endar felt he had achieved his revenge for all the fancied wrongs Hanlon (as Lona) had done or contemplated doing to him.

Satisfied for the time being, although not too happy at the situation in which he found himself, Hanlon withdrew his mind from the bird, and twisted his body into a more comfortable position on the bunk. There was so much he had to think about, and now that he was undisturbed was a splendid time.

He felt confident that the Ruler, Elus Amir, knew the truth about Adwal Irad and the conspiracy, and would no longer hesitate about joining the Federation.

"He might, though, at that," Hanlon thought seriously. "Especially if he happens to get it into his noggin that we Terrans were back of all that has happened. It's a dirty shame he doesn't understand us better—or that we don't know their ways of thinking better. But then, that's the cause of half the troubles between individuals, nations, races and worlds—they simply don't understand the basic motivations of the other fellow. But about Amir—I wonder if now isn't the time to prod him a bit? If—or as soon as—I get out of here, I'll try someway to get in touch with the Federation, and suggest we have the ambassadors come back and talk to him again. He ought to be ripe now."

It was only after some time that he remembered to wonder if Irad had been hurt or killed by his runaway caval. "I should have stayed in its mind until I knew if he got home or what."

Hanlon again sought out a bird, and when he was in control of its mind, sent it winging across the roofs and the countryside to the home of the Second-in-Line. When it got there, nothing could be seen to indicate that anyone was at home, nor was anyone visible when the bird peered through each of the windows.

Hanlon perched the bird on a tree limb while he thought seriously for some moments. Then he sent the bird on the Ovil Esbor's house. "Maybe I can pick up a clue there."

But as soon as the bird started looking through windows, Hanlon knew he had uncovered more than a clue. For Irad was there, talking to three or four men.

Hanlon wanted very much to hear their conversation. But how? The bird hunted in vain, but could find no open door or window by which it could enter. Nor were there open chimneys as are so common on Terran worlds, for the Estrellans covered their smoke-and-fume vents with fine screens.

Hanlon made the bird perch on a tree limb and go to sleep. Then he sent that portion of his mind from its brain, seeking some small animal, rodent or insect inside the house. He finally found one of their rat-things in its hole beneath the foundation. He took over its mind, wincing as he did so at the vicious, stark ferocity there. But he made it scamper through the walls until it came to the room where the conspirators were talking. The rat had already gnawed an entrance hole through the bottom of the wall there, and Hanlon had it crouch just inside, listening.

It took him only a few seconds to realize that the angry Irad must have told the others about their strange fiasco that morning, and that they were planning how they could finish the thing they had started.

"I don't dare go back to the palace, myself, for some time, at least," Irad scowled blackly. "I lost my head and gave the whole thing away back there…I know. Came right out and told Amir I was going to kill him. Who'd have guessed those fool cavals would act the way they did?"

"There's something mighty funny about that, Adwal," one of the men said in a puzzled tone that almost contained a hint of accusation. "One caval could quite easily have become frightened at something, or taken it into its silly head to bolt. You never can tame or train 'em completely. But you said all of your group did the same thing. That just doesn't sound right to me. What made them do it, just at the wrong time, and spoil your plans?"

Hanlon could hear the Second-in-Line laugh sneeringly. "You suggesting magic of some sort, Ovil?"

"I'm not suggesting anything—I'm just asking," and now the man's voice carried even more of suspicion and accusation. "It all sounds mighty strange and unbelievable to me. We'd like to know more about it."

There was a dangerous sharpness in Adwal Irad's voice. "Are you questioning the truth of my report, Esbor?"

"I'm not doubting you…yet. But there's something going on here that looks peculiar, to say the least, and we want to know all about it. That assassination was planned so carefully. And all the men with you were good riders. It just doesn't seem possible that all of them should have lost control of their cavals at exactly the same time. And that business about the animal Yllo was riding—throwing him and then killing him, as you reported."

Hanlon, through the rat's ears, could hear the other men muttering agreement to this.

Irad sprang to his feet, his voice shrill. "You calling me a liar, Esbor?"

"Not exactly, but I do think we deserve a better explanation of your failure than that silly story. We're all in this, too, and our lives are more at stake than yours, since you're Second…"

"You won't have to worry about your life any more," Irad screamed, and almost too swiftly to follow he yanked out his flamegun and cindered the politician's body before any of the others could object or stop him. As the man's body—what was left of it—fell to the floor, Irad swung his gun about menacingly, covering the others, who had risen in fright.

"Any of the rest of you phidis want to call me a liar?" he rasped.

"No, of course not, Adwal," one of them spoke in a placating manner. "We've never doubted you."

"Anybody with any sense could figure out that you really tried to kill Amir," another said. "Why, look. You're the one who started all this, and you sure wouldn't have worked so hard, or spent so much on this campaign, if you hadn't intended going through with it."

"That's right. What happened was just some tough luck. And Esbor was getting ideas that were bigger than he was. So let's forget what's passed, and settle down to planning something else, and making sure it's foolproof this time."

But Hanlon, disgusted as he was at the way they truckled to Irad, afraid of their skins, touched their minds and read the wonder they felt as to what had so changed Irad this past year. He had always been ambitious and, since being designated Second-in-Line, somewhat inclined to be dictatorial and overbearing.

But, their puzzled thoughts said, he had never been vicious, or displayed the killing instinct he was now showing. Too, his looks, his aging, worried them. They shook their heads with anxiety, as they began making new plans.

CHAPTER EIGHTEEN

IT WAS SOME TWO HOURS LATER WHEN Hanlon, in his own body, heard steps outside, and the sound of a key in his prison door. It opened, and one of the palace guard officers stood in the doorway.

"Well, you're awake," he said. "You sober now?"

"I never was drunk," Hanlon snapped, sitting erect to give his thought-out alibi. "I was working there in the stables, and felt myself getting faint. I managed to stagger into the tackroom, where I knew there was a cot—and that's all I remember until I found myself here."

"The head groom said you were drunk, and had us arrest you and bring you here. But you don't look like a man who had been dead drunk a few hours ago."

"Come smell my breath. You'll see I wasn't. In fact, I very seldom take even a drink of mild toxo and I haven't had any of that for many periods. Mykkyl's my drink."

The guard came close, sniffing, and Hanlon continued his prepared but necessary lie. "Ever since I was a boy I've been subject to these fainting spells. I'm getting so I can usually feel one coming on, and go lie down somewhere. In half an hour or so I wake up and am all right again until the next seizure. They usually come only two or three times a year."

The officer scratched his head. "Can't smell no liquor. Guess you must be telling the truth. In that case, there's no sense keeping you here. You can leave if you want to."

"Thanks, friend. I suppose it was a natural reaction, after seeing me unconscious."

Hanlon walked out of the little residence jail, and went back to his room in the groom's quarters. There he sat down to plan what his next moves would be.

"I've got to warn the Ruler some way, and make sure he is really protected," he thought. "But how can I do that? Maybe

166

he likes me well enough to promote me to a place in his guards. Oh if I could only talk to dad about all this. I need his help and advice. Dare I take the time to start hunting for him again? Or must I keep on working here?"

His heart clamored for him to do so, but he made himself consider every angle and connotation of his situation as coldly and logically as possible, as though the admiral was just that, and not also his beloved father.

He should, Hanlon supposed, warn the Ruler. On the other hand, he knew Amir was no fool, and that as a result of his near-death the past few hours, he would certainly be taking greater care of himself than ever? Incidentally, Hanlon wondered, how badly was Amir hurt?

Was there anything further he (Hanlon) could do about it?

He thought and thought, but could not see just how, without giving everything away. Perhaps he could get word to young Inver, to keep a more careful watch over his father. But trying that, too, would be a giveaway. Was it time for that? Time for him to come out into the open and appear as a Terran and a member of its Inter-Stellar Corps?

SSM George Hanlon had matured tremendously under all the experiences he had undergone since joining the secret service, but he was still only a very young man. Such problems as these were really far above him, he felt. They were things he simply did not have sense enough to figure out correctly. Not enough experience, not enough brains, he told himself with what he thought was an honest evaluation.

Nevertheless, he knew he was alone, that it was up to him, and that he had to make a decision one way or another.

But part of that decision was not left up to him. He was interrupted in the midst of his cogitations by the sudden opening of his room's door. He looked up in annoyance—and it was Endar.

"Pack your things and get out," the head groom said harshly. "I've seen the Ruler, told him about your disgraceful act of being drunk on duty, and have his permission to discharge you. He was very disappointed in you, he said."

Beneath his harshness Hanlon could easily detect the man's fierce satisfaction at having thus rid himself of a potential (as he thought) competitor. From his reading of the other's mind, Hanlon knew that Endar had *not* talked this over with the Ruler, and was doing it on his own. But the young SS man did not dare reveal his knowledge of that fact at this moment.

So he made himself say plaintively, "But I wasn't drunk. I felt one of my fainting spells coming on, and ran into the tackroom to lie down while it was on me."

"A trumped-up excuse, which doesn't help," Endar sneered. "Even if it was true, which I know it isn't, we don't want such people working here. So get out—and fast." He threw some money on the bed, as wages, and left.

In a way Hanlon was rather glad. It did help solve some of his problems, in that it left him freer to go and come where and when he wished. So he made no further protests, but silently packed his things, pocketed the money Endar had left, and went out and got his trike and rode back to Stearra. He wondered if his old rooms had yet been taken by someone else.

When he reached the building where he had been living, he parked his tricycle in the shed in the back yard, and went up to his old apartment.

The padlock and hasp had been forced, and the door was closed but unlocked. He opened it and went in just the same, for there were still some of his things there. He was determined to get them, even if someone else was living here now.

But the moment he got inside he sensed something changed. He stood quietly, letting his mind sniff at the feeling, trying to figure out what it was. He thought he heard a slight noise in the next room, and tiptoed softly across to the door. It was, he now saw, slightly ajar, and he peered through the crack. Someone was lying on his bed—an older Estrellan male, he judged by the longer, heavier beard.

Something about that face seemed familiar.

The being in the spaceship high above the surface of this planet had been growing more and more puzzled and unsure of itself during the past several days. Its plans seemed to be going all awry—and it was not quite sure why.

That native it had been controlling had not acted as he was supposed to act. Or rather, things had happened that had made it impossible for him to act always as directed. Even to the being the strange behavior of those four-legged beasts for riding, that had ruined its carefully prepared plan, was completely unexplainable.

And there was still the problem of that one unreadable mind on this world. Various things the being had done or caused to be done had enabled it, through its high-powered, multiphased scanner, to SEE the entity and keep track of its various goings and comings, but all its most intense efforts had not yet been able to touch that mind.

That this entity was working with those others who had such a different mind-texture from the usual run of Estrellans, it had long since proved to its satisfaction. The being now knew what these others were, and what they were trying to do on this planet. But who or what that unreadable entity was, what it was doing, and why—all this had so far defied the being's utmost powers.

So it was puzzled and as nearly worried as it was possible for one of its race to be. Also, for the first time during its very long life, the being was beginning to lose a little of its supreme faith in its own abilities. It was almost beginning to wonder if it was possible for itself to fail in its mission? But that was unthinkable.

And yet, it almost wailed mentally, that entity MUST be working toward the same ends as those others. Was it their master?

For nearly two Estrellan days and nights it had been considering carefully and minutely all the data so far acquired, and what its next actions should be. One thing it had early decided—there was no further use for confining or controlling those other two strange-minded creatures from that other system. It therefore released the "flee" compulsion from the one, and caused the "jailer" to open the doors and allow the other to leave its prison.

As George Hanlon stared at that figure on the bed, he reached out mentally and touched its mind. Instantly he let out a yell of delight, flung wider the door and ran to the bedside.

"Dad, you're free!"

Admiral Newton woke, saw his son, and pushed himself erect. But as he did so a grimace of pain crossed his face, and Hanlon was all solicitude.

"What's the matter, dad?"

"Guess I'm not in very good shape," his father managed to grin. "Been half-starved and tortured a bit. But never mind that now. I'm glad to see you. When I was freed, I figured the quickest way to find you was to come here and wait. Guessed you'd be back sometime."

"Just lucky I did. Things worked out a bit differently than I expected, or I might never have come back here."

He explained in short, terse sentences what he had been doing and what he thought he had accomplished so far.

"So you see, dad," he concluded, "why I'm doubly glad to see you, both because it means you're free; and so you can advise me what we're to do next."

"Hmmm," the admiral thought swiftly. "We've got to do something immediately, that's for sure. Of course I have the authority to approach Amir as a Terran, in case of need. But do you know for sure," he bent a penetrating gaze on the young man, "whether or not the Ruler has decided in our favor?"

"No," Hanlon said honestly. "I don't know that. But it seems as though he should have, now that he knows what Irad was trying to do, and why. If we go to him at once, and urge him properly, as well as explain why we are here and how we were trying to protect him, he should swing over our way. At least, that's what I'd about decided I ought to do."

The admiral was again silent, his brow creased in a deep frown of thought. Suddenly he snapped his fingers in decision, and looked up. "We'll do it. I have uniforms hidden in one of my hideouts here, and we'll get rid of our disguises and go see him."

He climbed from the bed, and Hanlon gasped as he saw how emaciated his father was, and the marks of his torture. But the admiral dressed, then both went down and climbed aboard Hanlon's motor-trike.

But when they got to Newton's room, another surprise awaited them. For Hooper was there, waiting for Newton as the admiral had waited for Hanlon.

After mutual exchanges of experience, the three thankfully began removing their Estrellan disguises, worn so long and so uncomfortably. Their clothing off, they jumped beneath the pipe-shower, and as the water softened the hair and plastic, they took off their false ears and noses, and ripped the hair from their bodies. Then they shaved their beards, and more or less trimmed each other's hair to the best of their ability.

"Boy, does this feel good?" Hanlon cavorted, naked, about the little room, while his father and Hooper laughed their own relief.

Admiral Newton pulled a large travelling-case from beneath his low bed, unlocked the three complicated and pickproof locks, and took out some uniforms. The others looked their astonishment, and he grinned. "Didn't know I had yours, too, did you?"

Clean, shaved and dressed in their uniforms, with the symbols of their ranks on the collars and shoulder tabs, the three sat comfortably in easy chairs, discussing plans and telling more fully what each had discovered.

Hanlon learned that the plot had been far more widespread than he realized. Almost every city on the planet had a cell working at the spreading of the propaganda against Estrella's joining the Terran Federation, and the lesser rumors about the insanity of Inver, the Ruler's son. He now learned the real reason for that whispering campaign, and wondered how he had missed it before. Inver stood Third-in-Line, and would become the Ruler after Amir if anything happened to Irad.

Both Hooper and Newton, who had worked more exclusively in other cities than Stearra, knew the names of most of the native

Estrellans who headed these cells, and they could be picked up and arrested when the time came. The crime wave had been quite widespread, also, as had the whispers that the Terrans were to blame for it.

The other two were loud in their praise of Hanlon's work in uncovering the real head of the plot, and his splendid work in saving the Ruler's life when his assassination had been so carefully planned.

It was noticeable that the junior SS man no longer took their praise with the cockiness he had formerly exhibited. In fact, he was actually apologetic and uncomfortable. He squirmed and blushed, and tried to minimize what he had done.

George Spencer Newton Hanlon, secret serviceman of the Inter-Stellar Corps, had finally grown up.

It was so late when they completed their plans that Admiral Newton decided they had best wait until morning before seeking an audience with the planetary ruler. Besides, he and Hooper both needed all the rest they could get, before embarking on any new campaign.

Hanlon prepared the best meal he could from the meager supplies in the admiral's room, and they all ate, then went to bed.

But deep down in his inner consciousness, a warning bell seemed to be ringing as George Hanlon lay in bed. It took him many long, anxious minutes of intense concentration before he was able to isolate the feeling from the many new items that had been talked about that evening. But he finally brought it into focus in his mind. He sat upright, disturbing his father, who was almost asleep.

"What's the matter, Spence?" sleepily.

"Amir," Hanlon said with agitation. "He ought not to be left unguarded like this. Those gangsters, led by Irad, are sure to make another attempt to kill him—and quickly, now that Irad has tipped his hand."

"But what can we do?" Hooper was also sitting up on the blanket-pallet that had been spread for him on the floor of this small, one-bed room.

"I...don't...know," Hanlon said slowly. "I...I can probably watch, through a bird or something, what's going on. But if they try anything..."

Newton started to climb out of bed. "I'll go notify the residence officials. Maybe we can alert his guards to be more watchful."

Hanlon was still worried. "I don't know about that, either. Maybe some of them have been planted by Irad...and if we say anything to the wrong ones it might merely hasten their plans."

"That sounds reasonable," Hooper said. "Irad would certainly never overlook a chance like that."

"If he could make it," Newton admitted, lying down again. "Maybe you'd better keep watch, Spence, since you know how. If you see anything starting, we'll do our darndest to break it up."

And in its spaceship the alien being awoke the Estrellan native it had been controlling for so long, and impressed certain commands on his mind— nor was the native able any longer to make any attempt, however feeble, to resist. Continued compulsion had at last weakened his will to the point where all suggestions and commands were instantly obeyed without question.

He therefore rose, dressed, equipped himself with a flamegun and certain other instruments, and left the house where he had been hiding out.

CHAPTER NINETEEN

ALTHOUGH GEORGE HANLON HAD BECOME adept at the use of the minds of birds, animals, fish, rodents and insects even at a considerable distance, he could not project his mind to any great length to find and gain control of such a mind, unless he had already used that mind and knew its texture and characteristics, or unless another part of his mind was already at that distant point in another brain.

Thus, in the present instance, he could not project his mind the many miles between his present location and the residence of the Ruler, Elus Amir, and find an animal or bird mind he could take over. He could have done it, that is, with one of the cavals he had at various times handled, but one of them could not get into the palace and the Ruler's suite. Nor could he locate any of the birds he had used out there.

He did, however, project his mind into Inver's caval—the one he had helped heal—and from that vantagepoint tried to find a bird he could control. But none seemed to be anywhere near the stables.

So, he had to start closer to where he was, and work outward. With time of the essence at the moment, a bird must be used. Just how he was to get a bird into the residence, and more or less keep it inconspicuous and unseen during his survey, was a problem that would have to be tackled when the time came.

Lying on the bed in the little room, therefore, he quested about the nearby neighborhood trees until he found a swift-flying bird he could use. It took but a moment to do so, and to take full and complete control of its mind and body. Then the bird, whose brain now contained as large a portion of Hanlon's mind as he could force into it, was winging at its top speed toward the official residence of Amir, the Ruler.

"The palace is in sight." Hanlon's voice was low but penetrant. Then after a time he said, "I'm looking for an open window or door."

The other men watched with amazement and intense curiosity as the young man lay there on the bed, his eyes closed and his face drawn with concentration, as they could see in the dim light of the shaded lamp Hooper had risen and lighted. Both of the other SS men knew much of what Hanlon could thus do, yet watching him do it was a new experience to both, and one that filled them with deepest wonder and a sort of awe.

The silence, even though of only two or three minutes duration, seemed like hours to the waiting watchers, then a jubilant "Ah!" let them know Hanlon had succeeded in the first part of his quest. "Got in through an open window in an upper story...heck, the door's shut."

Another pause, and then the voice continued, "Here's another. Hah, this one opens into a hallway. Now, which way is Amir's suite?"

They waited with impatience while they knew the bird Hanlon was controlling was seeking the proper portion of the interior of that great building. It seemed long and long before the soft voice spoke again.

"He must have gone to bed—the door is shut. I'll have to get outside and try again, but now that I know where it is I'll see if I can get directly into his room."

Hooper whispered in a tone he thought only Newton could hear. "By the shade of Snyder, but this is spooky. If I didn't know he could really do it, I'd swear it was impossible."

But only a portion of Hanlon's mind was in that distant avian brain. The rest was here in his own body, and heard the comment.

"Yeh," he drawled, "I know it's weird, and even I'm not used to thinking about it yet. Never thought how it would affect others. You don't need to whisper, though. The two parts of my mind are separate and distinct, so that I know what is going on in both...ah, one of the windows in the bedroom is opened, but only a crack. Maybe I can squeeze...did it, but I lost a few feathers. But I'm inside now. Let's see. There's a molding quite high up on the wall. It's wide enough so I can roost on that, sideways. Now we'll just have to wait and watch."

"Is Amir all right?" his father asked anxiously.

Hanlon grinned. "The way he's snoring he must be."

But the question reminded Hanlon that the Ruler had been wounded. He made the bird fly down to the bed, and through its eyes saw only a small bandage on one of Amir's arms—luckily for him the Ruler slept with his arms outside the covers. "Must be he got only a slight burn, after all," he said.

"Is there anyone close to his room—or can't you tell?" the admiral asked after a few moments of silence.

"I'll see if I can find out." Hanlon sent his mind questing out from the bird, and soon reported, "There're two men in an adjoining room…they're guards…from what I can read of their minds they're not thinking any seditious or murderous thoughts. Just playing a game of some sort while keeping on watch."

"Better keep checking them from time to time, though, hadn't you?" Hooper asked.

"Yeh, it'd be a good idea."

The other men were tired and not well, and despite their efforts to keep awake, dropped off to sleep. Surprisingly, even Hanlon's body and the main portion of his mind also lapsed into the unconsciousness of sleep. But the part in the bird kept awake—and so did the tiny thread of consciousness that connected it with Hanlon.

Some time later, about midnight, Hanlon, through the bird, heard a stirring sound in the anteroom, and investigated. The guard was being changed, and these two newcomers, he found from their minds, were tools of Irad.

Along that thread of thought sped the warning, and Hanlon's body and the balance of his mind came fully awake. He lay there for some time, studying the situation, but nothing seemed to be happening. He was almost back to sleep again—his body, that is—when the bird heard a fumbling at the door of Amir's room, although the sound was softly muted as though the one out there was using the utmost stealth in hopes of not being discovered. Hanlon's mind quickly investigated, and found only one mind there. Evidently the guards had left, for this was a new personality.

Hanlon reached out a hand and shook his father into wakefulness. "Someone's outside, trying to get Amir's door unlocked, or opened," he reported.

Newton called Hooper, who sat up, rubbing sleep from his eyes while the admiral explained in swift words.

"The door's locked from the inside, and the key is still in the lock," Hanlon told them. "I made the bird fly down and look…whoever is at it must be using something like pliers to try to turn the key."

Admiral Newton jumped out of bed, lit the lamp, and commanded Hooper, "Get up and dress. We'll have to rush out there." He turned to Hanlon. "Can you come with us, and still keep *en rapport* with your bird?"

"Sure," Hanlon was already throwing off the covers, and getting up. "The fellow, whoever he is, although I would imagine it might be Irad, is having trouble with the key, but he'll probably make it sooner or later."

"D'you suppose we can get out there in time?" Hooper asked.

"We'll certainly try," the admiral grunted, leaning down to fasten his shoes.

"Can you wake the Ruler?" he asked anxiously a few moments later. "He might have a better chance if awake."

"Sure," Hanlon said, and a moment later he followed with, "The bird flew down and brushed its wingtips across his face. He's awake now...he's sitting up...light the lamp...I sent the bird close to him then over to the door...he's watching it...now he sees the key turning...he's jumped out of bed...running to another door leading out of the room."

The three finished dressing and now ran from the room and down the stairs. Outside the admiral commanded, "Follow me..." He then ran toward the back of the house. They saw the dim outlines of a shed and a high-powered, family-sized touring tricycle. They piled into the seats even as the admiral was getting it started. Swiftly he backed the car out and into the street and then took off with a full-throated roar from the powerful, souped-up engine.

"Special job the Corps' experts fixed up for me," he explained as the others gasped at the unexpected speed.

Hanlon, through the bird's eyes, was still watching that distant effort to unlock the door and relaying to the others from time to time what he was seeing.

"Ah, it's unlocked...it's opening...but the Ruler is in the other room and has locked that door."

"The old boy's not so dumb," Hooper applauded.

"I'll say he isn't," Hanlon agreed joyfully. "He's plugging the keyhole."

He was silent a moment, then exclaimed, "The intruder's Irad, just as I thought it might be…he's surprised the Ruler isn't in bed…asleep…he gone over to try the other door…he's found it's locked and the keyhole plugged…he seems to have lost his head—he's pounding on that door, and yelling."

He half-straightened, then slumped down into his seat, and his face strained with concentration. Hooper, in the back seat, leaned forward and started to speak, but Newton restrained him. "Let him alone, Curt—he must be working on something difficult."

Hanlon was beating at the barriers in Adwal Irad's mind, trying to get in, even though he knew he had never been able to do so before. But it was all he could think of to do at the moment, and he had to do something. Besides, it was plain to him now that the man was completely insane—the way Irad was acting and the things he was saying and thinking showed it so clearly. So Hanlon had withdrawn entirely from the bird's mind, and was now working on Irad's with all his power.

The Second-in-Line had drawn his flamegun and was firing at the door, trying to burn out the lock or through the door panels.

Hanlon was almost in a frenzy of desperation. They had to stop this madman someway. He knew his father was pushing his car at its unexpected top speed, and that they would be there in a matter of minutes. But he was afraid that even those minutes might be too late. He did not see how they could possibly get there in time. For the door was beginning to burn from the fierce heat of the flamer.

Hanlon still beat at that barrier in Irad's mind. He seemed to sense somehow that it was weakening, was…was disintegrating… was changing horribly under the influence of hatred and the madness the man seemed to feel.

All this time the admiral had been trying to coax even more speed out of his souped-up tricycle, and now in the swiftly nearing distance they could see the few lights that denoted the residence. Soon they were close enough to see that the gates were closed.

"Those gates strong ones?" Newton asked without turning his head.

"No, mostly ornamental."

"Hang on, then, we're going through. Curt, grab the kid."

Hooper leaned forward, took hold of Hanlon's shoulders with his strong hands, and braced himself against the back of the front seat in which the younger man was sitting.

A couple of guards had run up to the gate at sight and sound of that speeding machine. But they ducked hastily back as they saw it was neither going to stop or swerve.

There was a rocking jolt, a crash, and the car was past the crumpled gates, careening wildly. The admiral fought the wheel with all his strength. By the time they came close to the steps leading up to the main entrance, he had it under control.

There was a screech of brakes that brought several attendants on the run through the door. The trike slid to a halt, and two of the three men in it jumped out and dashed up the stairs...

"The Ruler's being attacked," the admiral cried imperiously. "One of you show us his rooms."

A servant half-dazed by sight of those strangers in their peculiar uniforms, and subconsciously controlled by the command in Newton's voice, obeyed.

They raced across the entrance foyer to the great stairs that led to the upper story. Other servants were coming into the hallway, sleepily rubbing their eyes, and most of them only partially dressed. Their wondering eyes followed the racing men in a stupefied way, but none tried to stop the intruders.

"Down here." The servant dashed into a side hallway and the two secret servicemen pounded after him.

They turned another corner, and the servant slid to a stop. Two guards were standing there, flamers in their hands, menacing a small group of servants.

Newton took it all in with a single glance. From what Hanlon had said he knew the men were Irad's. "Burn those guards!" he snapped the command at Hooper, and the latter's blaster spoke twice—fierce blasts of death that made the flashes of the flameguns seem like candle flames. The two guards died instantly.

Newton and the servant were already dashing into Amir's bedroom.

Meanwhile, back in the machine where he had stayed, Hanlon was still working on Irad's mind. Now he thought he perceived a minute opening toward one edge of that decomposing barrier. He attacked it with all his mental strength, and it began to crumble a bit faster. Further and further Hanlon dug away at that tottering mentality until there was an orifice completely through the shield. Instantly he pushed his mind through...down and down, in and into the deeper parts of Irad's thoughts and memories.

And his body stiffened suddenly at what he found.

Newton and the servant pushed on ahead into the bedroom just in time to see the man, Irad, sink to the floor, writhing in apparent pain.

But even so there was still enough control in the maddened conspirator so that he swung his flamegun and sent a streak of fire flashing toward the intruders.

The servant, not expecting such a thing, and slow of reflexes, caught most of the blast, and died almost instantly. Newton, trained to quick action and always expecting the unexpected, ducked down and away. Even so, an edge of the flame caught him in the shoulder. The sudden, intolerable pain threw him off balance, and he sank to the floor his uninjured hand grasping the wound, trying to stanch the flow of blood.

George Hanlon was still in the tricycle, his mind a welter of conflicting emotions. He must be nuts—such a thing as he had just discovered was simply not possible.

"But it is," a cold, precise, soundless voice spoke in his mind. "It is not the mind of this Adwal Irad you are now contacting, but that of another, who has been controlling this entity for some time now."

"Who…who are you, then?" Hanlon gasped.

"I am from another, distant section of this galaxy, here on much the same errand as yourself and your assistants. I am banding together the various inhabited planets in my sector the same as your Federation is doing in yours. This planet is about midway between the two groups. I discovered it some time ago, and after thorough study of it decided to annex it to my oligarchy. But I have failed, and you have won."

"You mean you were responsible for all the opposition we've encountered?" Hanlon asked in surprise.

"That is correct. Working through the mind of this now-dying entity called Adwal Irad, I caused certain things to be done, including the increase in what you call crimes, in hopes they would alienate these people from your Federation's invitation, which was made shortly before I came here to work. It was my plan to make them join with me after denying you, and for certain things promised this Irad in the way of personal power, he more or less agreed—although I had to force him on several occasions."

"So that's why he changed so," Hanlon now knew the answers to many puzzles.

"Yes there was continual conflict in Irad's mind. It was conditioned to a love and loyalty for his world, and certain ethics of what he considered the fundamentals of right and wrong, that are totally unknown to me. In fact, these people are almost non-understandably different from the races in my oligarchy, but they have many resources I need. Thus the disturbance between what this Irad innately felt, and what I forced him to do, drove him insane. Even now his body is dead, and I am keeping his mind alive merely while I converse with you—a thing I have wished to do for long and long. I shall leave now, for my project has failed. I congratulate you on your victory."

There was a moment's hesitation, then the thought came again to Hanlon. "But there is one thing I would like to know before I go."

There was almost a trace of pleading, of indecision in that hitherto coldly logical, precise thought—and Hanlon wondered anew what sort of being this could possibly be with whom he was telepathing. For he could perceive nothing whatever as to the bodily shape or size of this enigmatic stranger.

"Why was I unable to make contact with your mind?" the alien asked, and its thoughts were almost a wail. "I perceive now that you are very young, very immature and inexperienced. I should have been able to read you easily. My abilities must be very small indeed, even though I have always considered myself so competent. Are you of a different race from those others with whom you worked? I know you are not a native of this planet, for your mind texture is far different from theirs, as is your fellows'. Even as yours, in some ways, differs from theirs."

"I honestly do not know the answer," Hanlon thought frankly. "I am of the same race as my companions, but I have some slight additional mental powers not usually found in my people. It may be I have a natural block or barrier in my mind they do not possess."

"It must be so. I could make no contact with you at all, whereas I could penetrate and control easily with the others. It is only now, while we are jointly tenanting this weaker mind, that I can converse with you through its brain—I still cannot do so directly. It is very puzzling..." And Hanlon felt the withdrawal of that mind.

Irad's body, now that the mind which had been keeping it not-dead, or semi-alive, had slumped to the floor in full death.

CHAPTER TWENTY

CAPTAIN GEORGE HANLON JUMPED FROM THE big tricycle and ran into the residence. None of the guards or servants tried to stop him, so dumb-founded were they by all that had been happening. Knowing the way from his controlling of the bird that had found Amir's rooms, Hanlon was soon there. He did not stop to see what was happening to the others, but ran across the bedroom to that far door, and rapped on it to attract the attention of the Ruler, hiding behind it.

"Everything is safe now, k'nyer," he called through the badly charred panels. "The assassin is dead. You can come out now."

"Is this some new trick?" a voice came thinly.

"No, sire, it is no trick, but the truth. You are safe now."

"Who are you?"

"I'm…" Hanlon started to give his name, then remembered that the Ruler did not know anything about him. He quickly changed it to, "I'm Ergo Lona, the groom with whom you talked on the ride the other morning."

"Lona? Where did you disappear to—and why?" suspiciously.

"Endar discharged me, but I have been watching over you, just the same. On my honor, k'nyer, you may believe me."

After some further hesitation there was the sound of the padding being removed from the keyhole, the insertion and turning of the key. As the door opened a mere crack, Elus Amir peered cautiously out. But instead of the clothing of a groom or a countryman, he saw the brilliant space-blue and silver of an Inter-Stellar Corps uniform.

He started to pull shut the door, but Hanlon had stuck the toe of his boot in it.

"It's all right, k'nyer. I am Lona, the groom. I am also George Hanlon, a captain in the Terran Inter-Stellar Corps. We discovered that another attempt was being made on your life, and were lucky enough to get here in time to block it."

He took hold of the edge of the door and pulled it open, for the Ruler was so surprised by this revelation that he made no real effort to hold it shut. Amir came slowly, surprisedly into the bedroom, staring keenly at Hanlon.

"You don't look like Lona…but the voice does seem to be the same. How does it happen the Federation has men here? Were you spying on me?"

"Not on you, sire, but on your enemies," Hanlon said earnestly. "Let me introduce you to Admiral New…"

He had half-turned back as he spoke, and now for the first time saw his father on the floor, a hand clutching his shoulder, from which a great stain of blood was drenching the uniform sleeve.

"Ring for your physician," Hanlon turned and commanded the Ruler. Then, realizing this was no way for him to be addressing a planetary head, he quickly but entreatingly added, "please, k'nyer."

Elus Amir called in one of the servants clustered outside, and commanded curtly, "Get the doctor here, immediately." Then he went over to the two on the floor. "Let me look," he half-pushed Hanlon aside, and stooped to peer closely at that wounded shoulder.

"Help me get him onto the bed," he said after a quick inspection. "I don't think any of the bone is gone—it's just a bad flesh burn."

Tenderly the two men raised the admiral, who protested weakly that he could get up by himself, and lifted him onto the bed. Amir himself began pulling off the admiral's tunic, while Hanlon helped.

By the time the doctor came running in, and took over the dressing of the wound, they had the arm and shoulder bared. But the elder Newton, in spite of his protestations, had fainted from the loss of blood and shock.

Amir sent the assembled servants away, retaining only his dresser, who helped him on with his day clothes.

The doctor worked swiftly, as Hanlon watched anxiously, applying ointments to the burn, and finally bandaging it.

"He's weak from all the blood he lost, and doesn't seem to have been in too good condition anyway," the doctor said at last. "I hope the man is strong enough to pull through."

"Then give him some plasma," Hanlon said frantically. "He needs it."

"I don't know what you mean." The doctor was bewildered by the word, for Hanlon had had to use the Terran word "plasma," not knowing any translation for it.

"A blood transfusion, then, or at least some glucose."

"I don't know anything about those, either...say, you're not an Estrellan, are you?"

"No, we're Terrans. You mean you folks don't know anything about giving one person's blood to another?"

"Sorry, but I've never heard of such a thing. How is it done?" The doctor was apparently more interested in this new idea than in the admiral's desperate condition.

Hanlon felt faint. He staggered away from the bedside without answering, and went into the anteroom, where Hooper stood talking to Inver and some other officials, who had heard the commotion and had come to see what it was all about.

Hooper saw Hanlon's haggard face, and knew something was wrong. "Were we too late?" he gasped.

"Oh no, we got Irad and saved Amir, but dad was blasted— shoulder. The doctor has fixed him up as best he can, but dad's in shock, and these backward fools never heard of plasma or blood transfusions."

Hooper jumped forward. "I can give a transfusion. What's your dad's blood type?" he asked as they hurried to the bedside.

"Same as mine," Hanlon was peeling off his coat as he spoke, his eyes lighting with relief.

Hooper rapped quick questions at the doctor, but the latter shook his head. More questions, and more negative answers, then Hooper turned disconsolately to Hanlon. "They don't even have anything I could use to give a transfusion; no hollow needles; not even hypodermics."

The doctor pulled on Hooper's arm. "Please, tell me what you mean by blood transfusions, and plasma. How do you give them? What for? And what did the other man mean when he said he had the same blood type as the wounded man?"

Hanlon went to sit beside his father's bedside, and sank into an apparent mood of despair.

Meanwhile, the Ruler had finished dressing, and with his son, Inver, went over to listen to what Major Hooper was telling the doctor.

"Will you please tell me what all is going on here?" Amir asked so plaintively that the SS man had trouble concealing a grin. But Hooper sobered instantly.

"The Federation's Inter-Stellar Corps, sire," he began his explanation, "found out about the fact that opposition to your desire to accept their invitation was becoming stronger—and dangerous to you and to the peace of your planet. They sent four of us here to study the situation and to protect you if possible. To do that it was necessary for us to disguise ourselves as natives of your world, so we could move about freely and unnoticed. That is why Captain Hanlon worked it so you would notice him, hire him as a servant of some sort here, and he would thus be able to watch over you and conditions in general from close at hand. We had found out that Adwal Irad was at the head of this opposition and crime wave, and that his plans included your death."

"But now you're all in uniform—and your disguises removed."

"Yes, k'nyer. We were planning to come as ourselves tomorrow—or rather, this morning—and seek an audience with you. We knew about the attempt to assassinate you that was made on your daily ride, and so were watching you more carefully than ever. When we saw Irad trying to get into your room, and his men he had planted in your guards keeping back the servants who wished to come to your assistance, we hurried here to help protect you. It was so apparent Irad was determined to complete the killing he failed at the other time."

Elus Amir, Ruler of Estrella, took that startling news with barely a tremor. He motioned them to a seat along the side of the bedroom, to continue his questioning.

The doctor was dismissed, although it was plain he wanted to stay and ask this Terran more about those strange and new methods of treating wounds.

So until dawn the Ruler and his son—now Second-in-Line following the death of Irad—sat talking to Major Hooper about the Federation of Planets, and the benefits Estrella would obtain from joining the other worlds.

"Such things as the advances in medicines in which your doctor is so interested, are but minor matters among the many we can and gladly will tell you if you wish," Hooper said.

The Corpsman was able to convince Amir of the falsity of the rumors and arguments Irad had spread, about how Estrella would lose her sovereignty if she joined, and that Terra would make slaves of her people.

"That is such a damnable thing to say, k'nyer," Hooper was almost angry, but very much in earnest. "You have only to send some trusted advisors to the various planets of the Federation—we will gladly furnish them transportation as we did before—and have them talk to the common people of any or all of our worlds. They will find that while we of Terra were the ones who developed space travel and sent people to colonize the first discovered and habitable planets, that the citizens of each world choose their own form of government, and that many of them are now even stronger than is Terra, the mother world. And there are peoples of several worlds who are natives and not Terrans or their descendants, whom we have not only not enslaved, but are helping to grow culturally so they may some day be advanced enough to join us as full-fledged equal members of the Federation, just as you, with your advanced civilization, were invited to do."

While all this conversation was going on in low tones across the room, George Hanlon sat by the side of his father's bed, almost in a trance, so deep was his concentration.

From what he had learned while breaking past the disintegrating barriers in Adwal Irad's mind, and from the techniques he had learned to apply in his previous excursions into other minds, he now found that, because his father was unconscious rather than merely asleep, he could, in a way, by-pass those barriers and get down into the depths of cell and gland in his father's mind and body, even though he could not fully penetrate the block into the memories, nor control the elder's actions.

Carefully Hanlon studied those depths, aided also by what he had learned in his healing of the caval, and from his intensive studies of human physiology and neurones and allied sciences. Using the totality of his admittedly meager knowledge, yet guided by things no human physician had so far learned, he at last began to trace the pattern of how human cells, tissues and nerves regenerated themselves, and how new blood leucocytes are made in the glands of the lymph and the spleen. He was able to trace the connectors between the minute organisms and the brain that directed their activities.

Then he set himself to the delicate task of activating those functions to begin and hasten the healing process.

Hour after hour he sat there, oblivious to all else taking place around him, his own body lolling almost lifelessly in the big chair while all his mental powers were engaged in the monumental and hitherto unheard-of task to which he had set himself.

The other three men concluded their conference at last, and got up, stretching hugely to pull themselves more awake after their half-night vigil.

Amir called in his servants, and ordered them to prepare and serve breakfast here for himself and his guests. Inver ran back to his own apartment to dress more completely for the day.

Hooper walked over to where Hanlon was sitting. "Asleep?" he half-whispered, doubtful because of the way the young man's body was sprawled in the deep chair.

George Hanlon stirred and sat up, flashing a smile. "You didn't need to whisper, Curt," he said. "I wasn't asleep. Just been helping dad get well."

The major stared at him in amazement. "What d'you mean?"

"You're half a doctor, Curt. Take a look at dad's wound."

Doubtfully, not fully understanding even yet what his companion meant, Hooper removed the bandage. He stared unbelievingly at the wounded shoulder. The deeper portions of that terrible burn were completely regenerated with healthy tissue. There was no sign of inflammation, no scarred tissue or fused flesh as usually shows in a fresh flamegun burn. The upper parts of the injury, too, were already beginning to heal toward the center.

"Why...why," he was astounded. "That should've taken weeks. I never knew a wound to heal that fast."

"I found out how to speed up the cells and things," Hanlon said simply.

Admiral Newton roused as they talked, perhaps at the touch of Hooper s gentle hands removing the bandage. Now he opened his eyes, and after a moment to realize his surroundings and recall the events of his injuries, smiled at his co-workers.

"Hi, fellows. Everything under control?"

"Yes, sir, all okay," Hooper answered. "I think the Ruler is about ready to sign up."

"Good. Good work. Say...I feel fine. No pain—yet I seem to have a memory of being blasted...of fainting." He frowned, then shrugged. "Couldn't have been much after all."

"It was very bad, sir," Hooper assured him gravely. "The burn was almost to the bone in your shoulder, and you lost a lot of blood. But now the wound is over half healed."

"Great John. How long was l out?"

"Only a few hours, dad," Hanlon said.

"Oh, you found the kit, then?"

"What kit?"

"There's a complete emergency medi-surgical kit under the seat in my tricycle."

"Now he tells us," Hooper spread his hands and spoke in mock despair.

"Probably just as well," Hanlon said. "If we'd known about that I might never have felt the necessity of discovering how to heal wounds as I did."

"What're you talking about?" the admiral looked from one to the other in perplexity.

"The kid's too modest to tell you, sir," Hooper broke in, ignoring Hanlon's signal to keep quiet. "I don't pretend to know how he did it, but somehow or other he managed, with his mind, to stimulate and speed up the healing, so that at the rate it's been going, your wound should be all well in another twenty-four hours. I'll bandage it up again, and then, unless you're too weak, you can get up and help us eat breakfast the Ruler is having sent up for us all."

Young Inver, who had returned to the bedroom, was standing there, listening to all this. Now his expressive eyes lighted up, and he touched Hanlon's arm. When the young SS man turned to face him, Inver breathlessly asked, "Was that the way my caval got well so fast?"

Hanlon grinned at him. "I knew it was your favorite mount, and I didn't want to see it destroyed."

He turned quickly back to help his father get up. The admiral found that, while he was still a little shaky, he could stand up without dizziness. The Ruler had sent his uniform jacket out to be cleaned and mended, and this Newton donned. Soon the men were seated about the table the servants had set up; eating the splendid breakfast they brought and served.

Meantime, the five talked about the problem that so much interested them all, and that meant so much to all the peoples of their worlds.

"Our Colonial and Survey Bureaus are constantly seeking throughout space for other planets having intelligent races, and we feel sure yours will not be the last we'll find," Admiral Newton told the Ruler and his son. "It is egotistical and silly to think we Terrans are the only civilized peoples in the universe."

"Chances are we'll find others who are as far ahead of us in intelligence, science and technologies as you Estrellans are ahead of us in ethics," Hanlon added honestly.

Amir and Inver looked up in astonishment at that simple statement. "You…you actually mean…honestly…that you Terrans do not believe you are the highest form of life in the universe?" Inver put their questioning into words.

"Great John, no!" Admiral Newton exploded. "Oh, I suppose," he added more slowly, "that there are some earth people who may still feel that way, but the majority of us do not, especially those who have traveled at all extensively. We used to think that; used to believe, hundreds of years ago, that we were the only intelligent life in the cosmos. But we know better now that we're spreading out. I, personally, have been on at least six planets that contain intelligent life that did not stem from Terra, although yours is the highest of the six, and none of the rest are yet at the point where they can be asked to affiliate with the Federation as equal members. But those others are being taught and coached as best we can—and as much as they want to be. In a few more generations they'll probably have reached the point where they will be ready to be seriously considered for equality status with us, as far as Federation membership is concerned."

"Just how do you determine the fitness of a race for membership in your Federation?" Inver leaned forward, his expressive eyes questioning. His father started to rebuke him for his forwardness, but the admiral interrupted.

"No, that's a good question, and we're glad to answer it—just as we're glad to answer *any* questions to which we know the answers. As to this one, we look first for signs of intelligence great enough to enable the people to govern themselves without continual warfare," he said earnestly. "Their knowledge of science and technology is not so important, we feel, although their ability to learn is. Some races will probably never have real need for machines of any sort—races like the plant-men of Algon, where Captain Hanlon was recently instrumental in freeing them from slavery."

He paused a moment to marshal his thoughts. "Then we look to see if they are making a conscious effort to advance in education and learning—no matter along what lines that may be," he continued. "We study their knowledge of and interest in ethical matters—their religion, and their belief in the general concept of right and wrong, of decency and observance of the rights of others. If they have these things, and have, above all, the desire and determination to continue their cultural growth, then we consider them worthy of equal Federation membership."

"And your wonderful people certainly measure up to all of those concepts," Hanlon added sincerely.

CHAPTER TWENTY-ONE

THE FIVE HAD FINISHED EATING BY NOW, AND the Ruler rose. "I will call my advisors together, and discuss this matter with them," he said. "But I can tell you now that I am more than ever disposed to accept your invitation. I could do so this moment," he said with a deprecating smile, "but I like to make sure that the leaders of my people agree with my decisions, as much as possible. I will have a servant show you to my study, where you can discuss your own plans while my ministers, my son and myself talk in the Council Chambers. I will let you know as soon as we reach a definite decision."

"Thank you, k'nyer. We will gladly await your answer," Admiral Newton rose, too, and bowed, as did Hanlon and Hooper.

"And thanks for the fine meal," Hanlon grinned. "I was really hungry."

Inver came up to him and laid his hand on Hanlon's shoulder. "I like you," he said simply but from the heart. "I hope we shall always be friends, and shall meet often through the coming years."

In the little study the three found easy chairs, and Admiral Newton turned first to Major Hooper. "As far as I know now, we'll all be going back when the sneakboat comes in a day or so. I suggest you go back to Simonides and get in touch with the High Command to get your next assignment."

"Right, sir, will do."

"About you, Spence, I want you to come with me and…"

"Excuse me, dad, but if I can have some free time, there is some very important research I want to do, that I think will benefit humanity much more than another detective assignment."

"What's on your mind, son?"

"This new ability I'm beginning to get," Hanlon said seriously. "I've found I can get down to the level of the body cells and glands, with my mind, and I think with more study and research I can learn things no one else has ever known before. But I'll need a lot of help from research doctors and endocrinologists, to tell me things I don't know. I may be all wet, but I have an idea I can, in time, make some very important contributions to medical science—with their help in telling me what to look for, and if it can be arranged so I can have the time to devote to that. I don't mean," he added, flushing with embarrassment, "that I think I'm..."

"You are, whether you think so or not," his father interrupted, eyes gleaming with pride and some amusement. "With those special gifts of yours, you can do things no one else ever hoped to do. Such research would certainly be worthwhile, especially if you can help others learn how to heal wounds as fast as you did mine."

"Speaking of which," Hooper broke in, "I suggest, admiral that you lie down while we're talking. It will be less strain on your body and heart, and you're still weak, even if you won't admit it," he added as he saw a protest forming on Newton's lips.

When Hanlon added his entreaties to Hooper's, the admiral grinned and lay down on a couch there in the study. "Anybody'd think you guys were the head men, not me," he growled, but good-naturedly.

Then he sobered quickly and went back to their discussion. "I'll have to take it up with the Board, of course, but I think they'll agree. I know of nothing definite needing you right at the moment, so they'll probably give you a leave of absence for that research."

"I'd like to go to some other planet than Terra or Simonides," Hanlon said. "One where I'm not known, so I won't have to be watching out for anyone who might recognize me. And if I'm to do the study, I'll want authorization to work at some of their insane asylums, too."

"Why those, in John's name?"

"When I tackled Irad's mind towards the end, I was able to get down inside of it, further than I've ever been in any other person's mind, because he was insane at the last, and his mind was breaking down. There seems to be a block or barrier in every sane person's mind that I can't get through."

"But you got into your father's..." Hooper looked puzzled.

"In dad's case, Curt, it was only because he was unconscious, rather than asleep or awake, that I could penetrate. Even then I had to sort of...well, by-pass the barrier...to get down deep enough to touch the cells and glands and such things. Of course, with more study and practice, now that I know more about it, I may be able to reach those depths in spite of the block...oh, heck, I sound like I considered myself a sort of superman," he flushed again, and his eyes implored them not to think him conceited.

"We know you neither are a superman nor think you are," his father assured him quickly. "You have a special gift, and you are trying to use it to benefit others, that's all. Don't be modest— it's really false modesty, in a way. Go ahead with your ideas."

"Well I'd also like to try working with engineers and technies, to see if it would be possible to rig up some sort of a mechanical method of doing the same thing."

Newton shook his head in puzzled wonder. "You're completely beyond understanding, Spence. I sometimes wonder if you're human...if you're really the son of Martha and myself."

"Why, no," Hanlon grinned then. "Didn't you know? I'm a changeling the little elves left on your doorstep."

His father and Hooper laughed away the tension. "Could be, at that," the admiral said. "Well I'll certainly recommend to the Board that they grant you all the time and opportunity you need. If you can get to the bottom of this, and especially if you can teach other doctors how to get at those glands and use them..."

"That'll be the hard part, dad. What I do hope to be able to do is to perhaps find out more exactly how the nerves and cells and glands work, and then doctors would be better able to diagnose and treat various diseases and injuries."

They were interrupted by Inver, who came in to ask certain questions the Ruler and advisors wished to know.

"Would it be possible, or rather, is it something you would permit," he asked, "for us to set up some sort of an advanced school or university here, and have you send us instructors? A place where our best young men and women could go to study the many things we know nothing about?"

"It certainly will be possible, and it is a wonderful idea," Admiral Newton assured him. "And one thing we want to make clear, that you do not yet seem sure of. That is that there is no question of our 'permitting' you to do what you want to do. None whatever, in any way, shape, or form. Your government is and will always be completely autonomous—always handled as you people see fit to work it. We never, under any circumstances, try to make other races 'conform' to any standards or regulations they do not wish to make their own. We will give freely of our knowledge, our science and technologies, our beliefs and concepts—but you Estrellans will be the sole and only judge of what you want to accept.

"And we will want to have you send some of your people to our universities, to teach us the advanced things you know that we don't. Your system of ethics, for instance, and the way you have learned to live together so closely and honestly."

After Inver had gone back to the conference the three men sat about waiting. Newton had almost fallen asleep—Hooper was completely so—when Hanlon stirred.

"I don't know, though," he ruminated aloud. "Maybe there's something else more important than that research at the moment."

"What?" his father roused himself sufficiently to ask.

"That alien being I contacted in Irad's mind."

"What in Snyder's name are you talking about?" Newton raised up in excitement. "What alien?"

"Oh that's right I didn't tell you. You're being hurt and my trying to heal you made me forget it." Hanlon explained swiftly about that strange mind and its startling communication.

Admiral Newton swung his feet to the floor, all thoughts of sleep banished.

"And you waited all this time to tell me a thing as important as that?" he demanded incredulously and almost angrily.

"Sorry, dad, I just happened to feel your life was more important at the moment, because the other could wait for a…"

"Okay, okay…I'll buy that for now. But we'll have to make other arrangements immediately. We'll have to find out where it came from and whether this other oligarchy or federation or whatever it is, is a menace to us."

"I don't think it is," Hanlon said slowly. "The being's mind was very peculiar, but it appeared to be extremely logical in its thoughts. It said that since it had lost and we have won here, it was withdrawing—and I don't believe it meant temporarily, either. I think it meant it was all through here and…"

"Don't be silly or childish, son," the admiral was intense and forceful. "That one being may have felt that way but his bosses won't. With two groups of planets so near in space—both with means of space travel—there's bound to be war of some sort, whether actual, ideological or economic remains to be seen. We'll have to hunt them up, and find out what it's all about—and immediately."

Hanlon shook his head. "I'll acknowledge your greater experience, dad, but I still have a feeling you're wrong about this. I believe that other race is entirely different in their way of thinking to ours—that they are coldly logical and not the type to keep on fighting for something they've already lost. But, of course," he shrugged, "its up to the High Command to decide. I'd still like to get on with that other research."

"I'll put both problems up to the Board," Newton said. "But I bet I know how they'll decide. There's the fact that those beings can read and control all our minds—except yours. It looks like your job, son—yours and no one else's...although we'll all be behind you in every way we can, of course. Meanwhile," stretching out on the couch again, "until Amir and his advisors want us, I think we'd both better take a nap."

"I am kinda pooped, at that," Hanlon said, and sprawled out in his chair.

The admiral was soon asleep, but only Hanlon's body and part of his mind relaxed. The balance of his mind was inside his father's body again, speeding the healing of that shoulder burn.

Finally Inver came to call the three Terrans into the Council Chamber. His broadly smiling face, and the thoughts Hanlon read from the surface of his mind, told him the decision had been favorable—a fact he signaled to the others at once.

"We are completely convinced now," Elus Amir told them when the Terrans were seated about the conference table, "that our world will be best served by joining your Federation as we were asked to do. If you have the treaty papers at hand, I will gladly sign them. And my son," looking proudly at young Inver, "will sign with me as the next Ruler of Szstruyyah."

"We do not have the proper documents," Admiral Newton said. "But our ship will be here tomorrow night, and it has long-range communicators with which I will immediately get in touch with the Federation Council, who will send accredited ambassadors here at once. They should be here within five days."

"Now that we have made up our minds, we are anxious to affiliate with the other worlds. We feel it is a tremendous honor, being the first non-Terran race asked to join them."

"As it is an honor for us to have such a high-principled peoples joined to us," Admiral Newton said with a courtly bow. "May I suggest, k'nyer and nyers, that when our ambassadors arrive, you ask them for whatever help you desire in the way of teachers, goods or materials. They will gladly explain what we have to offer, and I know they will study you and your people to find the things they will ask for in exchange. Remember always, please, that it is our steadfast policy to teach only what you really want to know, and which you specifically ask for, not what we might 'think you ought to know'."

"That one thing alone," Elus Amir said, deeply moved as were the members of his Council, "would be enough to confirm us in our belief that we will be doing the right thing for our people in joining you."

Amir, his son and the councilors, rose and bowed. The three Terrans had also risen, and saluted punctiliously. Then Newton stepped forward impulsively and held out his hand, which Amir grasped as though he had always used the gesture.

"Welcome to the Federation of Planets, sire," Newton's voice was filled with emotion.

The Ruler silently wrung his hand.

When it was time for the Corpsmen to leave, after some general conversation between them all, the Ruler and his son were again profuse in their gratitude for what the men had done, personally, to save Amir's life, and the peace of their world.

They escorted the three downstairs and out to Newton's tricycle, and stood at Estrellan salute as the Terrans got into their machine.

"Oh one thing, Lona," the Ruler came forward just as Hanlon was getting in. Amir's eyes were filled with puzzled wonderment. "How did you know Adwal Irad was coming to attack me while I was asleep, locked in my room?"

Hanlon's eyes danced, but he kept his face straight. "We have a saying on Terra, k'nyer, that explains it—'a little bird told me'."

And he bowed again as he entered the machine, and Admiral Newton drove away, leaving behind a more than ever puzzled Ruler of the soon-to-be newest member of the Federation of Planets.

THE END

If you've enjoyed this book, you will not want to miss these terrific titles...

ARMCHAIR MYSTERY & SCIENCE FICTION CLASSICS
$12.95 each

If you've enjoyed this book, you will not want to miss these terrific titles…

ARMCHAIR SCI-FI & HORROR DOUBLE NOVELS, $12.95 each

D-121 **THE GENIUS BEASTS** by Frederik Pohl
THIS WORLD IS TABOO by Murray Leinster

D-122 **THE COSMIC LOOTERS** by Edmond Hamilton
WANDL THE INVADER by Ray Cummings

D-123 **ROBOT MEN OF BUBBLE CITY** by Rog Phillips
DRAGON ARMY by William Morrison

D-124 **LAND BEYOND THE LENS** by S. J. Byrne
DIPLOMAT-AT-ARMS by Keith Laumer

D-125 **VOYAGE OF THE ASTEROID, THE** by Laurence Manning
REVOLT OF THE OUTWORLDS by Milton Lesser

D-126 **OUTLAW IN THE SKY** by Chester S. Geier
LEGACY FROM MARS by Raymond Z. Gallun

D-127 **THE GREAT FLYING SAUCER INVASION** by Geoff St. Reynard
THE BIG TIME by Fritz Leiber

D-128 **MIRAGE FOR PLANET X** by Stanley Mullen
POLICE YOUR PLANET by Lester del Rey

D-129 **THE BRAIN SINNERS** by Alan E. Nourse
DEATH FROM THE SKIES by A. Hyatt Verrill

D-139 **CRY CHAOS** by Dwight V. Swain
THE DOOR THROUGH SPACE By Marion Zimmer Bradley

ARMCHAIR SCIENCE FICTION CLASSICS, $12.95 each

C-55 **UNDER THE TRIPLE SUNS**
by Stanton A. Coblentz

C-56 **STONE FROM THE GREEN STAR**
by Jack Williamson

C-57 **ALIEN MINDS**
by E. Everett Evans

ARMCHAIR MASTERS OF SCIENCE FICTION SERIES, $16.95 each

G-13 **SCIENCE FICTION GEMS, Vol. Seven**
Jack Vance and others

G-14 **HORROR GEMS, Vol. Seven**
Robert Bloch and others

www.ingramcontent.com/pod-product-compliance
Lightning Source LLC
Chambersburg PA
CBHW030324180626
46810CB00003B/1222